THE WHITE PALAZZO

the *White*
PALAZZO

A NOVEL BY

Ellen Cooney

COFFEE HOUSE PRESS
2002

COFFEE HOUSE PRESS is an independent nonprofit literary publisher supported in part by a grant provided by the Minnesota State Arts Board, through an appropriation by the Minnesota State Legislature, and in part by a grant from the National Endowment for the Arts. Support has also been provided by Athwin Foundation; Beim Foundation; the Bush Foundation; Buuck Family Foundation; Elmer L. & Eleanor J. Andersen Foundation; Lerner Family Foundation; McKnight Foundation; Patrick and Aimee Butler Family Foundation; The St. Paul Companies Foundation, Inc.; the law firm of Schwegman, Lundberg, Woessner & Kluth, P.A.; Star Tribune Foundation; Target, Marshall Field's, and Mervyn's with support from the Target Foundation; James R. Thorpe; Wells Fargo Foundation Minnesota; West Group; Archie & Bertha Walker Foundation; Woessner-Freeman Family Foundation; and many individual donors. To you and our many readers across the country, we send our thanks for your continuing support.

COFFEE HOUSE PRESS books are available to the trade through our primary distributor, Consortium Book Sales & Distribution, 1045 Westgate Drive, Saint Paul, MN 55114. For personal orders, catalogs, or other information, write to: Coffee House Press, 27 North Fourth Street, Suite 400, Minneapolis, MN 55401.

LIBRARY OF CONGRESS CATALOGING-IN-PUBLICATION DATA

Cooney, Ellen
  The white palazzo : a novel / by Ellen Cooney
    p. cm.
  ISBN 1-56689-134-5 (pbk. : alk. paper)
  1. Automobile travel—Fiction. 2. Young women—Fiction. 3. Lesbians—Fiction.
  4. Psychics—Fiction. 1 Title

PS3553.O5788 W48 2002
813'.54—DC21   2002071280

FIRST EDITION
1   3   5   7   9   10   8   6   4   2

PRINTED IN CANADA

To Chris Fischbach

"The more we speak of Fortune's ways, the more we find to talk about, in all fair justice to Her. It's no wonder that, if we seriously consider this, we see that everything we foolishly call our own is really in Her hands, shifted from one to the other and back again, in a way we can never understand. This fact is fully brought to light every single day, in every possible thing, and though it's been proved in other stories, I will add one of my own."

—Boccaccio, *Decameron*

One

Tara Barlow made a list of what to do next, and four things were
on it:

> Quit my job!
> Leave Mom and Dad a good-bye note!
> Pick somewhere to go!
> Cancel the real estate!

She was not in shock although it seemed so. She knew she wasn't
in shock because people in shock have glazed-over eyes and feel
stupefied. Her eyes were wide open. She was twenty-four years old
and she felt that, if there was ever a person who knew their own
mind, it was her.

If she couldn't have her wedding reception at White Cliffs, no
way would she get married, not to Tommy, not to anyone, not
soon, not ever, no *way*.

"Sweetheart," he said, "it's unbelievable that the wedding place
you picked burned down, but we still have four months and we love
each other, so let's go find another restaurant!"

Tara had it in her to rise to the challenge of the fire just fine. It
was only the beginning of September. The date of the wedding was
in the middle of January, and she wouldn't lose money on a deposit.
The Gallaghers of White Cliffs knew her well: they didn't even ask

for her credit card number to book the wide, shiny banquet hall. And the invitations weren't printed yet, so there wasn't the problem of expensive cards directing one hundred people to a restaurant that was no longer there, like a wedding invitation in a nightmare.

When she stood in the road at the bottom of White Cliffs Hill and looked up at what the fire had done, she could have flung herself to the ground in a beautiful fit of passion and cried like a cloudburst. Drying her eyes on the backs of her hands, she could have squared back her shoulders and got on with it, as if that's what really mattered, getting on with it, as if she'd be just as well off with a wedding at the steak house near the highway, with statues of cows in the lobby and a DJ playing Fleetwood Mac, Chicago, oldies like "Ain't No Mountain High Enough," and hits from the soundtrack of *Grease*.

There was no other restaurant. There was only White Cliffs.

She was calling everything off, and she could not care less if no one understood her point of view. She felt that everyone she knew, and everyone she'd ever met, could only think about things simplistically, in a one-dimensional way, like four-year-olds, as if the personalities of everyone around her had stopped developing when they were four years old. If she wanted to talk to someone who was willing to admit that, yes, life was full of strange complications, strange troubles, strange desires, and heights and depths and shadings of things that were not always visible on the surface, and not always easy to explain, who was there?

She could talk to the air. She could get into her car and close the windows and talk to her car. There was no one to talk to.

She had a Mustang, eight months old and red like a fire engine. No one drove it except herself and it was barely broken in and all paid for. The seats were light-brown crinkled leather, like expensive couches, not cheap, stick-to-your-skin, clammy vinyl. She paid

THE WHITE PALAZZO

extra for the good upholstery. She felt that the engine was like a young, strong heart, without imperfections. She had never played a piano, but every time she clutched, she felt that this was how it worked to pump a pedal.

The dealer had tried to sell her an automatic transmission because she was a girl—Bozo Johnson at the Ford place, he came right out and said it, "Tara, you're a girl, quit looking at the manuals," as if you had to be a guy to drive a stick. She had thought of girls in a history book, sitting on horses sideways, where they swung themselves over the side of a horse as if, instead of two legs, they had one, as if their thighs were glued together. Only a mermaid, she felt, would have a reason to ride a horse sideways. If she'd lived in those days and had a horse—a Mustang—she would have climbed in the saddle with the seat between her legs. If she ended up in jail for it, she'd feel that the ride had been worth it.

"I'll go west," she decided. "I'll go west like the setting sun."

A general direction wasn't hard. North was out of the question: with anything north, it would soon be winter. She wanted nothing to do with extra weeks of winter, and she didn't want to take the time to pack her winter clothes.

East and south were no good. Her town was in a valley in central Massachusetts. When she crossed the river on the old stone bridge to the highway, then around the hills, she could only go two hours straight east, or three straight south, on less than half a tank of gas, before stopping in her tracks at the Atlantic Ocean itself, or some harbor or bay. She'd find herself out at a ledge, about to drive off a cliff into foamy, gray waves, like Thelma and Louise, but in the sea.

She made a note to herself to add something else to her list. "Make sure with the good-bye note to Mom and Dad, I don't make it sound like I'm killing myself."

She had always wanted a winter wedding. There didn't have to be snow, just cold, with a world outside the White Cliffs windows that was hard and cold and hostile, while inside, where her party was, it was glowing. New snow would have pushed it over the edge from being nice to being perfect, not that her hopes were ever up, unrealistically, for new snow.

Like winter itself, her wedding was supposed to have four basic colors: white, silver, red, and green.

She'd bought her dress in the bridal shop at the mall, an ordinary bride's dress, chiffon. She couldn't call it a gown because it came from the regular section, not the "Tall." It only went down to her shins.

She never expected anyone to pat her on the back about the rest of her outfit. She was ready for complaints, and when complaints poured in, from home, from work, from everywhere, she ignored them.

"Tara, no one wears emerald high heels with a wedding gown."

"You can't wear your pewter necklace because it takes up all your neck and it looks like a collar for a dog."

"We respect your right to be original, but please wear normal eye shadow, not that slutty silver glitter, and put the blonde back into your hair before the wedding, because you can't get married bleached out."

"Honey, do whatever you want. I love the red pantyhose, but if you wear a red bra, it can't show. That dress is real white and real thin. Your boobs will look like two fantastic tomatoes, and no one can see you with red boobs but me."

What she liked most of all was to imagine the two opposing forces of herself in her outfit and the background of beautiful old White Cliffs. If she fixed herself up like a normal bride, she'd be in there like any other bride who had ever spent a great deal of money for a four-hour White Cliffs rental. She wanted to be in there as if she belonged there, as if she owned it.

She had imagined her wedding so often, and in so much detail, she'd have the strange sensation that instead of looking forward to the future, she was looking back at the past, as if the wedding had taken place already. She'd rearrange another part of the plans, like how many minutes the piano player should play before taking a break, and it would frighten her to think that, when the real thing finally happened, she might experience it too objectively, with an unnatural detachment: she might find herself walking around at her own reception in a daze, wondering if everything was in a memory, somehow, or in a dream.

She had wanted to be alert and awake, so everything would be clear and sharp, as if lit up with neon that would never burn out.

She thought of her memory as a bag or a pot or a tube. At the start of her reception, it would be filled with empty space; then her eyes would take in marvelous things.

From the moment the wedding was over, and the last of her guests went away from the lights of White Cliffs, into cold winter dusk, her bag or pot or tube would be loaded, for all time.

Was this a great way to start out in married life, with the feeling that the best thing that could happen to her would have happened already? Sometimes she had the feeling that all she wanted was a wedding, not a marriage. Sometimes she wondered if everything else that took place in her life would only make impressions on a not-deep part of her brain, where she attended to things that seemed important, but were not. Was she basically saying, "After the wedding, I'll have nothing else to look forward to, but maybe that's all right?"

But all she'd have to do was say the words "my wedding," and it would all come rushing in. The backs of her eyes would fill up with details. A piano player in a tuxedo would play songs that did not have words, and the hall chandeliers from France would glitter away, with hot white bulbs shaped like icicles. On a table in the lobby there'd be complimentary matchbooks with white covers and fancy black lettering that said,

White Cliffs
Banquets Our Specialty
In the Heart of Massachusetts!
Enjoy old-world charm at your function!

There'd be mistletoe in the White Cliffs doorways, and spruce and juniper laid out as thick as blankets along the shiny, polished White Cliffs hallways. No one would get drunk on the one allowed glass of champagne or on the spiced apple punch, in beautiful glass bowls, spiked only a little with rum, and so what if her parents and Tommy's whole family felt that she'd be out of her mind to not serve beer, because a wedding without beer was like a swimming pool without the water. If Tommy's friends tried sneaking in a cooler and hiding it in the men's room, they'd get thrown out the door on their arses.

The fireplaces would blaze like a scene on a Christmas card. There'd be platters of roast beef and turkey on huge silver trays; gravy in silver tureens; white tablecloths, white napkins, and centerpieces on all the tables of shiny, wild green holly, with fat red berries, looking good enough to eat. She had hesitated about the centerpieces because holly berries are poisonous. But she wanted that red and that green, even if it meant cards in the arrangements that said, "Do Not Put Into Your Mouth."

The fire took place in the middle of the night. It was just after Labor Day; the summer had been long and hot and too dry. Back in June, the long fields of grass had turned to straw, all yellow and brittle, like stiff, dry old brooms.

The fields were flattened like plates. At the top of the hill were cinders, ashes, dust. Instead of filmy autumn haze and the eastern face of White Cliffs, high and broad and beautiful, there was a cloud of gray-black smoke, and it seemed to Tara that the sky itself had been on fire.

There was the fact of the fire, and the burned, black-gray earth. There was the rubble of a big charred wreck, still wet from the firehoses, and still steaming. At the bottom of White Cliffs Hill, Tara shivered as if her skin had been touched with an ice cube. She wished she had a hat, but she didn't begrudge herself her new haircut. She'd done it herself and it was almost a crew-cut. She'd dyed it white, really white: she'd wanted to match her hair with her dress. The style was like a shorter version of Andy Warhol's wig. The leftover smoke made everything colder. The air was gray like iron, and it was filled with smells of burning, as if the fire were still taking place, but in a noiseless, dry way, like rust. White Cliffs Hill looked suddenly small, as if the sky had moved down closer. Not even one small part of a wall was left standing. There was nothing to point to and identify, such as, "that used to be part of the roof," or "that's an oak panel from the hallway."

Everything would be all right, he kept saying. He'd get on it right away. He wanted her to cheer up, to look on the bright side. "Look on the bright side!" he said, but he didn't say what that was, except that they'd find another restaurant, no problem. Then they'd go into their future all resilient and wise, with the sense of over-coming an obstacle, as if the fire were a hurdle in a race.

In the cold light of day, the top of the hill was as black and gray as an x-ray, where before there had been a perfect restaurant, with pillars and arches and beautiful wood, and windows in every room that were taller and wider than doors.

"Dear Mom and Dad."

She only needed to write one note. Everything she was leaving behind could be taken care of at once, including the real estate people.

"Dear Mom and Dad, I'm not freaked out about the fire but guess what! This is excellent! I love you, I'm not doing anything stupid, you have totally got to know I want to be *by myself* and I haven't got time to explain but I'm moving! Remember the Beatles song you hated about the girl leaving home and every time it came on the radio you turned it off and told me, *never do that to us,* and I said, *how could I?* So I'm not! This is not like 'She's Leaving Home' and if you think so, YOU WILL BE WRONG BECAUSE I LOVE YOU. Don't worry! If I find out you worried, I'll be so mad! Tell Tommy, 'Cancel your tuxedo, Tom, because she's calling everything off.' (He'll know why.) Thanks! If Work calls, if they notice I'm not there, say, 'She quit,' but make them send my last paycheck in the mail. Forge my signature and keep it! If the real estate people come looking for me, tell them, no deals! I'm still a fantastic daughter so *trust* me."

She and Tommy had been looking at houses and had narrowed it down to four. One was a ranch in the southern corner of town near the river. One was a split-level, to the north, very contemporary, like two ranches pushed together at two different levels of a hill. The third was a colonial at the end of West Hill Road, where all she'd have to do to see the sun go down would be to look out a window or stand on her own front porch. The fourth was a ranch to the east, near the highway, with great stretches of open road for a view of sunrises, and lots of open space. She hadn't been worried about competing with other buyers for the houses: she'd put down deposits on all four.

"Tara, make up your mind, just go eenie meenie miney moe," was something she'd been hearing from Tommy a lot.

He worked downtown at the bank that was just downstairs from her company, and he was very worried about the money she'd laid out, like money in a Monopoly game, he had felt. He had already started talking to the bank lawyers to help her get back those three other deposits.

Lately, she'd been leaning toward picking the split-level, facing west. But that was when the only fire she knew about was the one in the sky at sunset.

Two

"Gone," she started saying, the way a child tries out a new word. "Gone, gone, gone." One was for White Cliffs, one was for herself, one was for Tommy, and one was for the wedding that would never be.

She always arranged things in fours. She imagined that her mind, like everyone else's, had a built-in, personalized compass, with an actual magnetic field and four main points.

Her N was White Cliffs on its hill outside town, like a mansion.

For s she had the sharpest bend of the river, near a stand of weeping willows, where the water rose up, every April or May, and gushed and turned frothy and swirly, as if springtime made it think it was an ocean.

For w she had a real western point: the sunset on hot summer days, exactly down to the center of bare, bald West Hill, the lowest of the hills of the valley. At every summer dusk it would light up neon-orange, like a volcano in reverse, and the light and colors and fiery streaks would go down into the top of West Hill like lava poured out of the sky, through a funnel. For E she had the crystallized, gray-white sunrise of early fall, when the air was cooling down, and the first light of day wasn't filled anymore with heat and dust.

At her N, the hayfields were there too, below and all around White Cliffs, and even in winter the yellow grasses were tall in

THE WHITE PALAZZO

their fields. When the wind blew, everything leaned over and started swaying, like fields of grasses bowing.

There was never a time in her life when she did not have these feelings about White Cliffs. There was no first time she ever saw it, just as there was no first time she ever saw her own hands, or the river that ran along the edge of her town, or sunlight.

At her N it was always winter: there was snow but it was powdery. It was always just about twilight, and the front door of White Cliffs was always in the act of being opened. Light from the hall chandeliers poured out into the shadows, and the windows were incredibly clear, like rectangular plates of water.

White Cliffs, the river, sunrise, sunset. How could he not have known this? His eyes were looking at the same thing her eyes saw, but he could have been a hundred miles away.

"Let's go find another restaurant."

She had tried to fool herself that he was talking to her in code. Sometimes, in the window of the bank where his desk was, when they were newly engaged, Tommy made signs for her, which he propped up on his desk.

Flags, he called them. They looked like printouts from the web site of a company that serviced banks. He designed them himself. They said things like, "Finally Underwriters Can Know Many Elements To Assure Rates, Accounts." And, "Yearly Outcomes Unambiguous, Rates Priced Unilaterally, Savings Stupendous Yearly. Walk-in Offers Welcome!" She must have walked by those "flags" a dozen times without understanding what they meant. Then one day he told her, "Tara, it's codes, just read the capital letters and see what I spelled."

She had loved it that she was not the kind of person a fiancé would go to the Hallmark store for, and buy a tacky little sentimental card. She had loved it that the person she planned to marry looked so normal, in his banker's suit and his shiny leather pointed grown-up-guy shoes; and under the surface he was always doing something to surprise her. She had thought she would only ever get from him the sorts of surprises that thrilled her and made her blush.

But this time he hadn't been talking to her in code. How could she make sense of "Let's go find another restaurant?" If the watch on his wrist had started talking to her, or if the smoke in the sky had formed letters and words, like something coming out of an airplane, or from the broom of the witch in *The Wizard of Oz,* she would not have been more amazed.

"Tara, I know how you feel," he didn't say. "There is a hole where your N was, and this is very bad. I am the guy you're going to marry, so I know how you feel *exactly.*"

He did not come toward her in the place inside where she felt that a hole had opened up. How could someone be with you in a way-inside part of yourself, where no one else had ever been, and you think it's a permanent thing that they are there, and then suddenly, in one second, with just a couple of words, they show you that they were never with you at all?

All along, they were really outside you, in the ordinary, exterior world? On the face of her compass, where had Tommy been? At the place where the needle holds on. "Tommy, at the stem," she had thought.

They'd been engaged for three years, which Tommy had thought was too long, but the fourth year of their engagement, she had felt, would be the right time to marry. And she'd be just the right age, twenty-four.

"Gone, gone, gone, gone." This was for the four houses she had imagined herself living in.

"Gone, gone, gone, gone." This was for the four colors she would never have at her wedding.

And once more. "Gone, gone, gone, gone," for her bosses, at Fillins.

It was easy to imagine what they'd be saying about her. The four partners would call her a weakling and a traitor for not showing up and quitting her job face to face, but she knew what would happen if she walked in there. They'd try to get her to swear to stay with them forever, and when she wouldn't, they'd clutch at their chests as if dying. They'd remind her how good she had it with them, and they'd mention nice things they had done for her, such as, "Remember when you begged us to fix you up with Tommy Ernst?"

She remembered. It was the one big personal favor they'd ever done for her, and they would never let her hear the end of it.

Fillins Associates had a monopoly on temporary general employment placements. Their roomy, handsome public office above the bank was nicer than the bank, and much more bankerly. It was all mahogany, with creamy-colored wallpaper, with a feel in the air of a hush, as though something solemn was always about to take place.

When Tara started working for the partners, they did not put her in the front office, but in the back, and that was where she had stayed. It was a small outer room with its own set of back stairs. It must have been part of a vault when the building was new and the bank took up the whole building. For a desk, she had a Formica-topped table with rusty chrome legs that one of the partners had bought at a yard sale for about four dollars. For file cabinets she had thirty-two old-fashioned metal milk crates, which another of the partners got free, when a dairy in the valley went bankrupt. The crates were stacked on their sides in four columns, filled with tan folders, one stack in each corner of the room, at N, S, E, W.

The thing she cared about most in her office was the rug, and she knew that she would miss it.

Her rug was an indoor-outdoor carpet remnant left over from when the bank redid its lobby. She'd gone down there and salvaged it herself. She'd been watching the installers and knew there'd be a section left over. It had seemed like a good chance to strike up a conversation with the new new-accounts guy, Tommy Ernst. He had a desk just off the lobby.

She had found it astonishing that, coming in and going out of the building at different times of the day, it was necessary to walk through the lobby or pause on the sidewalk in front, by the center of the big plate-glass window where, on the other side, Tommy was at his desk.

Once, by the entrance, she misjudged where the door was. Reaching for what she thought was the handle, she bumped into the security guard, Dan Balboa, a Fillins temp she'd recruited from the Honda dealer who sold her her first car. Dan was short and squat, like a wrestler. He'd been wasting himself washing Hondas all day and riding in back seats when the dealer took certain types of people for test drives.

Tara slammed into him. She grabbed him by the arm and yanked at him, and he shook her off and cried out, quite forgetting himself, "Fuck off me! Fuck off!"

She cried, "I thought you were the door, Dan!"

Tommy Ernst looked up and she thought he'd tell her to be quiet, like a librarian would. But he said, "Excuse me, if you ever get arrested, do you have someone to go down and bail you out?"

"That's none of your business." She couldn't think of anything else to say. She felt that her eyes were out of focus. She felt that she was back in school, taking tests.

She didn't know much about Tommy, but she already knew what kind of car he had: the car was a problem. It was a predictable, dark-blue Toyota, a Camry, square in body and unimaginative under the

THE WHITE PALAZZO

hood. She had always felt that a person who'd drive this type of car was saying, "On top of being normal, I have no character."

His height was something she was willing to make a concession for. She was willing to change the decision she'd made a long time ago to never become attracted to someone short. Before she noticed Tommy in the window, she'd felt repulsed by tall women who marry really short men. She'd felt that she could never go through her life with someone who, every time she turned to face him, at home, in public, everywhere, well, the top of his head would be only as high as, say, her shoulders. She had thought she should not have a husband whose face was level with her breasts.

She didn't have to see Tommy standing up to know he was shorter than she was, by a lot. But she already liked how she felt when she was somewhere near him, even if "near him" meant standing in the lobby, or outside on the sidewalk.

She went downstairs to the bank and took the carpet remnant. It was rolled like a tube. It was standing upright in the corner.

He said, "Excuse me, are you stealing that?"

"None of your business." She couldn't have opened a new account because she already had two, a savings and a checking, in that bank.

There was only one thing to be done, and anyway, she felt that the partners owed her something big.

The partners were so cheap that, when they wanted file-photos of new potential temps, they expected Tara to pay for the developing, and she had to use an old Instamatic that made everyone look like they were standing in a lineup at the police station—even more so, for some of them, than they had looked when they actually were.

They gave her no expense account. When orientation sessions went four, five hours at a time, such as the weekend specials on topics like "how to never let anyone know that this is the first time you have ever signed a tax form," the partners wouldn't give her petty cash, not even enough for a soda and small fries at Burger King. When she asked for more money, they said, "You get a great salary, and you live with your parents and you don't pay rent, which we know about because we asked them."

Sometimes she was embarrassed by how simple it was to do her job. All she had to do was watch out for the right sort of person to start talking to. She knew where to look: at the mall and in the downtown shops and bars, and the paths along the river, where people went who had nothing to do, and the video stores and the pizza places and Burger King, and Wendy's and McDonald's, and the parking lot of Wal-Mart.

Sometimes she liked to compare her job to something mysterious and inexplicable, like poking at the ground to find water with a stick.

The best recruits were the ones who had husbands or wives with real jobs and benefits that covered partners. The second best were the ones who had something wrong with them, such as, they were one-legged, or sometimes dropped into clinics for drug treatments, and the government paid their health insurance. Third best were the ones who didn't know much English.

The valley was full of aliens and sometimes Tara went out with a focus: she'd spend a week talking only to Mexicans, or ten days in the lounge of the big Chinese restaurant near the mall. Fillins would never rely on just the big-account clients, not when there was a price to be paid from hospitals and restaurants and motels on every dishwasher, laundry person, and maid. They didn't let her inside Wal-Mart. She had stolen three stockers from them the day they opened, and a cashier the next week. She wondered if there might have been photos of her in the Wal-Mart offices, as if she were a shoplifter. Someone in a suit always came running towards her if she tried to walk in.

It was the same in the plastics factory, even though it was only next door. Her parents waved to her from their machines, not to say hello, but to tell her to go away. "Sweetheart, if you recruit one more person from here, they will cut off your hands, then they'll dick around with our retirement package to get even, so please don't come back." It used to be interesting to get into the factory when they'd finished a computer training course with their new office people. It was a very good course, very comprehensive.

There was only one rule Tara followed, and she'd designed it herself: she would never make promises that were completely removed from reality. If she put a client in a job cleaning toilets, she didn't say, "I lined up a great place for you as a sanitary engineer." She said, "The job I'm sending you to is full of shit, but it's temporary." And she'd say, "Remind me to invite you to my wedding, roast beef and everything, at White Cliffs."

She went into Fillins as a weekend-and-after-school temp herself, halfway through her sophomore year. She never worked anywhere else. On the Monday that followed graduation, she switched to full time. By the time she turned twenty-one, she was an old hand at getting the partners to pay attention to her.

She'd been twenty-one years old for two days on the morning when the partners—Betty Axelrod, Dave Weeks, Dave Bonnetti, and Ronald Coppenrath—came to work to find a message from her on each of their desks. The message was set up like a memo. On the "from" line it said, "TB, like the disease." They hated it when she did this because it reminded them that she was daring and mocking and young and strong, and they weren't, and her skin was shiny like a perfect piece of fruit, and theirs wasn't. But "TB like the disease" was what she called herself at work when she wanted to make a point.

On the "to" line were her nicknames for the partners. Betty Axelrod was "Ax." Dave Weeks was "Wee." Dave Bonnetti was "Bone." Ron Coppenrath was "Robocop."

Even if the partners *had* remembered her twenty-first birthday, they would have thought of a way of using it to save money. "Tara, it's Secretaries' Day next week, hee hee ha ha, so we'll give you one present to cover both, chocolate, perfume, flowers, a necklace, you name it."

The partners wanted their clients to imagine that crowds of potential employees were always waiting in the wings, as if the office were a stage, and the partners sat around like directors having auditions.

Fillins' temps were supposed to be the cream of the valley. Fillins promised its clients, especially the big ones in business, county government, schools, and expensive specialty shops at the mall, polite, reliable, deep-resume, extremely experienced temporary help. The partners didn't want potential employers of their clients to know that they had their own recruiter, so they hid her. "Tara Barlow, Staff Secretary," was what they called her.

The brass nameplate on her door said, "T.B., Staph Secret." It was a proper nameplate, very official, and she'd designed, ordered, and paid for it herself. No one from outside ever saw it except new recruits, who sometimes pointed to it and smiled.

She recruited, she oriented. Sometimes for long stretches, all she'd do was drive around the valley towns, looking at people who'd been out of work for a long time, including people who'd been out of work always. She'd wonder sometimes at the end of a day, "Why am I so depressed?" Then for days at a time she'd stay in her office with new clients, talking about "office techniques you need to know," and "things to be aware of if we put you at a cash register in like, Sears."

The partners would never allow her to become a partner herself because all she'd ever done for an education was graduate from high school. She signed up one fall at the state college in the next town for a night class—"General Psychology I." She felt brave about it. She had not done well in school; she had always done badly on tests. She'd choke up, staring at questions as if they were coded, and just when some words blinked into focus, the time would be up.

She suspected that she'd gotten away with a lot in high school because of the partners: on the day she graduated, she learned that a note from Fillins was on her permanent record, saying, "Whatever she does, pass her, we are waiting for her with a full-time job."

On the first night of her college class, she walked into the class-room with a notebook in her hand, like a six-year-old. The rows of desks were almost filled, but at the front, where a teacher should have been, there was a wide-screen, brand-new television, like at the bars.

No one had told Tara that her college teacher would be a tele-vision. Everyone else was sitting there, waiting, not talking, not looking at each other, with their backs up straight and their eyes on the big blank screen: who would turn it on?

She never even made it to a desk. She ran down the hall and out of the building to her car. The car was her first one, a little white two-door Honda. It wasn't new, but it was zippy, very light, and very friendly. She'd bought it with Fillins money as soon as she'd got her license.

The partners thought she'd changed her mind about getting a college degree because she had no self-discipline, no ambition. She didn't care what the partners thought.

TO: AX, WEE, BONE, & ROBOCOP

FROM: TB, LIKE THE DISEASE

THANKS FOR THE GREAT 21, PARTNERS! I WILL NEVER FORGET IT!

I LOVE TO WORK HERE SO MUCH! THE GIFT WAS GREAT!

STAY JUST AS SWEET AS YOU ARE!

Their reactions to her memo were predictable. First it was, "Don't be leaving things like this lying around in public in the *office,*" and "I thought we already told you to never write us anything again."

Then they were sorry, they didn't do it on purpose. They were middleaged, they forgot things all the time, birthdays, everything; she couldn't imagine what it was like to be them, in their suits, in their repressive, bad-for-you, nine-to-five, overly organized little orbits. Then it was, "Christ Almighty, what do you want? What can we do to make it up to you?"

What did she *want?*

"There's this guy downstairs," she told them. "I need a little help with pulling strings, because I think I want a date with him."

She couldn't confide in the partners anything about the longer-term state of her plans, such as, "Partners, I'm going to have a wedding at White Cliffs, and everyone I ever placed in a job, if they're still around, I'm inviting them." The partners thought White Cliffs was pretentious and moldy, with bad plumbing and boring, over-priced food. They never took clients to lunch there.

They never told Tara what strings they pulled, but it had worked. For her first date with Tommy Ernst, where had he wanted to go?

White Cliffs. She told him, "Another time," and they went instead to a bad, fake-Italian chain place near the mall. She ate overcooked rigatoni with clam sauce out of a can, and got sick in the parking lot.

THE WHITE PALAZZO

It did not end romantically. Tommy held her shoulders while she threw up. On their second date, the next night, at midnight, they went to a town farther up the valley to see *The Rocky Horror Picture Show.*

When they came out of the movie, Tommy told her he was glad she'd turned down White Cliffs. He'd only suggested it because it was so expensive. He'd wanted to make a memorable impression on her. The truth was, he explained, he'd always felt that there was something creepy about White Cliffs, and now, in his mind, it was just like the mansion in that movie, but with white New England clapboard and pillars. That was when Tara told him about her compass.

When she explained very carefully about her N, he covered his face with his hands, and groaned as if he'd been punched, and said, "I could change my mind about that restaurant."

On their third date, they got engaged. The throwing-up date was a Friday night, *Rocky Horror* and the description of her compass were on Saturday, and then, around noon, on Sunday, Tara woke up in Tommy Ernst's bed.

It was the first time she'd spent a night away from home. She had not been the type of child who had friends and got invited to sleepovers. She had never been to camp. And it was no good getting invited to stay over at houses of her relatives. Everyone she was related to either lived in the Johnson Street projects or in projects in other towns near other factories, all of them the same.

The Ernsts had a split-level brick ranch in the nice part of town, near the park and the broad, attractive town square, full of elms and oaks and maples and bushes and flower beds. No one had grit from dusty, burned plastic in their houses, clothes, hair, and eyes.

When Tommy wanted his own apartment, he went to the new high-rise off the highway, near the new computer companies in their nice, clean office parks, with views of woodlots and the river. When Tommy needed furniture, his parents said, "Oh, take everything you want from right here, we'll redecorate."

When she woke up with Tommy that Sunday morning, she stood up and stretched and sighed, and he was lying there looking up at her and saying, "Let's get married."

"ok," Tara answered. "But first, let's go to the mall."

He thought she was taking him out to breakfast to celebrate their engagement, but she took him to a shop called "Tie One On." It was a tie store. She found a counter with a sign that said, "Nautical Knits & Silks."

The tie she bought for Tommy was dark blue and had a row from top to bottom of gold-colored sextants. No, she wasn't buying it because she was trying to tell him that she wanted to go out with him on boats, and no, she wouldn't feel hurt because it wasn't the sort of tie he'd wear to work: the only designs the bank allowed on ties were geometric, and you couldn't have circles, just lines, stripes, or little diamonds.

The sextants were the closest thing the shop had to compasses. The sextants were purely symbolic. She was trying to tell him that she wanted to make sure he understood what she was talking about when she told him about her compass. She wanted him to know it was important that no one had known these things about her before.

She quizzed him: would he always remember where her east was, her west, her south? And her n, did he know what it meant to her to have that n?

He said he did. "I get it, I get it, I get it, I *get* it," he said.

"Well, you don't have to wear the tie to work," said Tara. "You don't even have to take it out of the bag. You can save it, then wear it with your tux when we get married."

It did not occur to Tara, at the time when this was happening, to wonder if it might have been a little unusual that she went out on her very first date, threw up, went to the movies, talked about her compass for the first time ever, made love for the very first time, went shopping, and got engaged, just like that, in one weekend. All she could do was hand the tie to Tommy.

Outside the tie shop, he made a vow. She knew that it was a vow because that was what he called it. "Listen to this vow," said Tommy. "I swear on my own two eyes that if I ever do anything wrong about your compass, which I won't, you should leave me. Just get up and walk away, and I hope I'm struck blind or something, because that's what I would deserve."

She didn't wonder what would happen to the tie. She didn't wish he'd take it out of his drawer and strangle himself with it. She felt no animosity toward Tommy. What would be the use of animosity? No stirrings of temper were aroused in her, no *anything*. She felt perfectly calm. He knew nothing about her at all. Now that this fact was clear to her, she knew what had to be done.

Three

It was the middle of the day but no one saw her go. Her parents were at work next door; no one was hanging around outside.

Her gas tank was full. Her tires didn't need air. Her engine didn't need oil. Her water levels were perfect.

She didn't own a suitcase. She'd never needed one. She took the pillowcase off her pillow and filled it with the contents of her top bureau drawer: socks, underwear, a few T-shirts, one pair of white sweatpants cut off at the knees to make shorts, and an old gray zip-front sweatshirt cut off at the neckline, where there used to be a hood. This was all that would fit in her pillowcase. She slung it on her shoulder like Santa Claus. In her bottom drawer was four hundred forty dollars, her own private petty-cash stash, and she took that, too.

"Bye!" said Tara, and she didn't care that there was no one to hear her.

Home was so small.

The rowhouses of Johnson Street were a mile and a half from the downtown shops, but they were off in a world of their own. With their flat roofs and old gray bricks, they stood like big cartons around a parking lot in the shadows of the plastics factory. There were four separate blocks of apartments.

They looked like bunkers in a fort or a compound, with eight gray front doors in each row, and eight gray identical stoops. The rows were numbered, although no one knew why, for the four main points of a clock. Starting with the block in the front, they went clockwise: Block Six, Block Nine, Block Twelve, Block Three.

The front windows and stoops faced the parking lot directly, on purpose, the way windows around a pond face a pond.

In Tara's rearview mirror, the buildings of home looked like four rows of dominoes. Her bedroom window, in the middle of Block Twelve, was less than the size of a dot. It didn't matter anymore that the window looked out on a solid brick wall of the factory, and could never be clean, and could never be opened, not even with a screen, because particles of pulverized, burned-plastic dust would rush in.

Now the factory smokestacks disappeared. The highway on-ramp sloped up before her in a wide, slow arc. The woods between the road and the river were thick with oaks. A light, swirly fog was in the air. She didn't expect to see the water.

There were other rivers in the world, and they were bound to be better than this one. This one was dirty and dull, and full of who knew what from the factory. The water was yellowy-brown. In a book she'd read at school, there was a description of pea soup. She was surprised to learn it meant fog. "Pea" meant the vegetable. Pee soup was what everyone in the valley called the river. No one ever went into it, not even in motorboats.

But just before Tara left it, a streak of river came leaping up between the trees like a big healthy fish, all flat and silver and shiny, showing itself in a flash, and she stuck her head out the window and cried out, "Bye, you stupid river!"

Along the rim of the valley, the hills started shrinking away, bottoms first, as if sinking. All her life, she'd known those hills as well as the walls of her own room.

"Bye, you dumb-ass hills!"

She headed west. Trees began to go by in long, high, evergreen blurs that were bundled with fog, as if someone dropped big bales of gauze from an airplane, and it all broke loose and got caught in the branches. It was woodsy for a very long time. She felt like a girl in a fairy tale, riding off into a forest of staunch New England hemlock, spruce, and fir.

Tara patted her dashboard. She wondered what it must have been like to be the first person in automaking history to have thought of putting a v-8 engine in a small, low car. "My little v-8," she called it. That was as close as she'd come to giving it a name. "My little v-8, like the juice."

She didn't believe in naming cars. In her first year of high school, there was a senior boy she took an interest in. The boy had a Thunderbird with a perfect body, from when Thunderbirds were in their prime, all pointy and rounded combined, with that growly Thunderbird *vroom*. The body was salmon-pink, with a white leather interior. It wasn't all precious and fragile like other old-time classics that, you spend a fortune on them, and the only place to drive them to was car shows. She'd never want to own an antique car, but she had loved to look at this one. The boy really took care of it.

But after she started paying closer attention to the boy, she found that he'd named his car for the princess in *Star Wars*. He'd stand by the parking lot after school with his keys in his hand and when a girl walked by, he'd say, "Lay ya! Lay ya! Lay ya!" He said it as if he sparkled with wit and originality. "Hey Princess! Lay ya!" When a teacher walked by, he'd say, somberly, "I was talking to my car."

That had done it for Tara in terms of going on a date in high school. Afterward, all she did was go to work, until the day she looked in the window of the bank.

"Don't think about him," she said to herself, and then, "don't think."

THE WHITE PALAZZO

She didn't have a CD player in the Mustang, just the radio and a tape player, which she never used. She didn't have any tapes with her. She wished she did. The only stations that came in on the radio were whiny, let's-get-drunk-on-a-twelve-pack, completely commercialized country-western. Everything else was static or talk shows with ten people yelling at each other at once, and those Jesus stations, where they said things like, "We know from our suffering that God is not fair in human dealings, so the question to ask as Christians is, if God is not fair, why should I be?" This was what they were talking about the one time Tara tried to tune in some stations.

She said out loud, talking back, "God is fair!"

She kept driving. It wasn't quite twilight, but it was definitely getting darker. The highway kept stretching and dipping and rolling. The hills to the west were much larger than at home.

She had to be careful. Her speed was under control. She couldn't open up on a state-run road, where someone in a shiny black Mustang was like blood in the water to a shark, if the police out here were like sharks, which they probably were, not like in the valley where everyone knew her. Thick clouds of low fog started making their way from the east, from a river that, compared to the one at home, was like water rushing out of a hydrant. The river at home was like drips from a leaky old sink tap.

The fog had nowhere to go. It was massing up in the west, against the hills, and forming high, white, impenetrable hills of its own. In front of Tara's eyes the hills doubled, became mountains, and kept growing. She started to get a little nervous. Soon the long miles of woods gave way to rolling fields, and farmhouses, and cows, cows, and more cows.

She didn't have a map. She'd never needed one before. She'd had her compass. It never occurred to her to buy a map.

She told herself that everything was going to be all right. There was herself. There was a road. There were wheels below her that were turning. She had pointed her car in the direction of the sun, and just because she couldn't see it in all that fog, she knew where it was; she knew that it was up there.

She started singing the first thing she thought of. She sang out, at the top of her lungs, "Oh, the farmer in the dell! The farmer in the dell!" But in the time it took her to draw breath for a really big belting of "hi ho the dairy-o," the spirit went out of her voice, the way water stops flowing from a crinkled or stepped-on hose, and comes out in leftover drops.

"Hi ho the dairy-o," Tara whispered.

No way was she heading straight west into mountains and fog.

She turned off the highway onto one of the old truck roads that passed through actual towns. Up ahead, there were streetlights like in a normal place to live. Streetlights broke up darkness and they also broke up fog. Streetlights! She could not believe that there were people in the world who could live without streetlights, completely rurally, when fog was balling up all around them like cotton, as if life in the country was like life in the bottom of a jar, and someone just stuffed in some cotton.

She passed by strip malls that double-sided the road. There were video stores, Taco Bell, a supermarket, a Chinese take-out with no tables, a Chinese eat-in with a lounge, a McDonald's, and a surf 'n' turf restaurant in a fixed-up barn, with a huge painted sign on the roof.

She slowed down to look at that restaurant. There weren't any lights, there was no sign of life, and it was hard to tell, with all that barn-board, if the restaurant was closed for the day, or for forever. It wouldn't have mattered. She'd never eat there: she would never eat a meal in a barn. But she loved that sign.

THE WHITE PALAZZO

It was almost the size of a screen in a drive-in. It was a sign of two opposites: a lobster and a burger were posed together. The lobster was cooked and red and shiny, and the burger was in a bun, well-done, with some red on the edge that of course would have to be ketchup. The lobster was four feet tall, standing upright on its tail, and it was leaning down toward the passive, much smaller burger. Dramatically, the lobster held out a claw, as if to offer the burger a handshake, as if to say, "Even though we're opposites, let's get along and work together like a team."

Tara felt that the lobster had a real personality and a mind of its own. It was reaching for the burger aggressively. If the sign came to life, the lobster would grab that burger and, with a big, nut-cracker-like pinch, it would fling it off the roof to kingdom come.

She was rooting for the lobster. This was not what anyone would expect in a restaurant surrounded by farms. Tara felt that this sign was a *sign*.

And she realized that this was the farthest away from the Atlantic Ocean she'd ever been, and she realized that, sooner or later, she would have to stop driving.

In a rational way, she made up her mind that the first motel she came to after the sign, she'd check in.

The first one was a Super 8, which would have been perfect, but it was next door to a Wal-Mart. Even if the window curtains were made of lead, she would not get a minute of sleep. The next one didn't count either. It had a sign on a pole that also held a blue electric bug zapper. "Pioneer Moto Court." If there ever was an "r" on the second word, it had fallen off a long time ago.

Tara cried out, to the motel, "You look like the one in *Psycho!*"

After about four and a half miles, the road veered off around a curve to the north. Another motel was set off the road at the end of a well-paved driveway. The office in the front had lights on, and their door was open. There were big leafy oaks out in back, and beyond the oaks were pine trees. She could smell them.

It was shaped just like home. She had left one set of blocks for another, but this one was full of colors, and no one knew her. The building had three sides, all connected. It had white aluminum siding and a flat roof and it was all on one level. It bordered three sides of the parking lot in the shape of an upside-down, straight-edged u.

The rooms in the u were numbered one to eleven, in order. Every room had its own outside light. Every door was the color of a popsicle. The paint was far from new but the colors really stood out: lime, cherry, grape, orange, lemon, root beer, and that shade of turquoise that's not a flavor, just a color.

The sign on the front was wood and paint, not neon, but it would do. Hathaway's Motor Lodge! AAA Discounts! We have cable! Full service kitchenettes! Come on in!

She went in. She began to imagine herself as a creature in a shell at the bottom of the sea, as loaded with spunk as that lobster. She imagined that her old life was a shell she had just crawled out of. She felt brave and adventurous. Right away, she began to think about how she'd start making some money.

Without too much effort, she let everything and everyone she'd known before simply slide off the edge of her mind into nothingness.

She liked the Hathaway. She made friends with the owners, and stayed there. And that was where, five weeks later, on a Saturday morning, at the peak of fall foliage and scenic splendors, as the brochures in a rack on the wall proclaimed, Guida Santucci walked in the door, and found her.

Four

Guida Santucci's little house was just outside town, on the road to White Cliffs.

On the morning after the White Cliffs fire, she woke in the same sort of panic an animal would feel, to the terrible smell of something burning. It wasn't one of her neighbors burning yard debris, normally and illegally, and it wasn't the yeasty, burned-wheat smell from the cereal factory by the river, and it wasn't something nasty from the smokestacks of the plastics factory, which were always getting out of hand. Guida crept to her bedroom window and looked out.

Where White Cliffs used to be, and all over the top of the hill, there was a dark, gray-black cloud, like the smoke of a bombed-out hill in a war. If the sky were like the map of America, the cloud would be as large as all of New England, with Pennsylvania and New York added on.

Guida had slept through the night of the fire like a stone in a pit of oblivion. Even worse, she had not seen it coming ahead of time, not even one small glimmer in the back of her mind, or one tiny, flickering spark.

If it were any other building, it would not have mattered that she'd not seen it burning ahead of time.

White Cliffs! It was the same to her as if she'd jumped out of bed and found that her own heart had gone away from her, as if it were sitting in a glass of water on her bureau with her partial plate of artificial teeth. But unlike the teeth, she'd never get it back into her body.

It was the biggest fire the valley had ever had. There'd been chaos and shouting and sirens, and the roar of the flames, and roaring water rushing out of hoses, and roaring wood walls that had crashed into bits on the ground. Every town with a fire station had sent over their whole department.

But Guida had not heard one siren or the rumble of a truck. She'd seen *nothing*.

She walked over there. Fire trucks were parked every which way on the hill, as if the blaze might start up again, although nothing was left; the firemen in their black rubber coats looked strange and sinister. People were crowding the road but she did not have the heart that morning to deal with people.

In a little crowd, halfway up the hill, were the owners of White Cliffs, the Gallaghers. Guida knew them, although they weren't customers of hers. They were huddled closely together, eight or nine of them, the whole family, with their heads bowed, and they looked like a painting in church of the crucifixion, as if the firemen were Roman soldiers with spears in their hands instead of hoses and axes. Their faces were soaked with tears. People had said forty years ago that the Gallaghers were crazy to have bought the old Sable mansion, never mind turn it into a fancy restaurant that ninety percent of the valley could not afford.

The Gallaghers had always been good neighbors. They never offered Guida a free meal when she went walking through the fields, or went inside, just to look around, just to be there, but they always offered her a glass of brandy. The fact that they didn't have a public bar didn't mean they didn't really have a bar.

Everything the Gallaghers had must have been inside that building. If a Gallagher had spotted Guida, and had come to her

THE WHITE PALAZZO

for a few words of hope, she would have found nothing to say, not even with lying.

She stood in the road at the bottom of White Cliffs Hill with her hands in her pockets and her elbows poking out. When someone jostled her, she jostled them back. When someone came over to her and said, "Signora, do you think it was arson," or, "Signora, come and visit me for dinner tonight," she hunched up her shoulders, looked at the ground, and said, "Get the Christ in hell away from me before I spit." This was not how she usually talked.

She was the only fortune-teller in the valley who did seeings, and the only one she'd ever heard of, anywhere, both in modern times and the past, who made house calls. She knew how much appearances mattered. Today, for the first time ever, she'd left her house without looking in a mirror.

There were two things Guida was afraid of. As for everything else, all she had to do was say, "Well, I have three eyes," and everything else would be canceled, the same way that, when the ugly little good-for-nothing crabapple tree in her yard burst into bloom, it canceled out how much she didn't like that tree. It was an eyesore, it cast pointy, unhealthy-looking shadows, and its fruit was so dry, even the crows wouldn't eat it. She'd feel the urge in March or April to go to the hardware store for something to chop it down with, and then suddenly, one morning in May, she'd look out the window at perfect pink blossoms, and act as if she'd never seen a flower before. Pink blossoms! They amazed her. This happened every spring.

She had a pear tree, too, a stunted, dwarf pear tree, as though someone had tried a long time ago to make it a bonsai, but they had only succeeded a little. If it weren't for the pears, and there really were pears every year, but small ones, that tree would not have been allowed to keep living. The crows were fond of the pears.

There were a great many crows in Guida's neighborhood and they felt that they had the right to do whatever they wanted. If she upset them, they'd probably grow in numbers, and start hanging around her roof, her electric wires, her telephone pole, like in *The Birds,* just as they'd do to anyone else who crossed them, except that Guida's house would be a house where this sort of thing would be noticed.

But that's not what frightened her. One of her fears, the minor one, was that she'd stop caring what she looked like.

Her clothes would be the first thing to go, then her teeth. She'd accidentally-on-purpose shrink her sweaters in a sink of hot water. Her skirts would never be hung on hangers. Her silk dresses and scarves and linen jackets would never go out to be cleaned: they'd get thrown in a pile of laundry with her underwear.

It would all go downhill from there, and soon, having lost all control, she'd be switching to denim and sweatpants, and then she'd look just like most of her customers. She'd go out of the house without her plate in, and the several gaps in her upper row of teeth would make her look like anyone's idea of someone you should run from.

The other one of her fears had to do with her extra eye and it was something she could not say out loud. But the truth was, several times, in the days before the White Cliffs fire, late at night, she fell asleep with the wrong sorts of questions in her head. "What if? What if all of a sudden? One day? The worst thing that could happen? What if it?" She was careful to never finish the words to these questions. But what if all of a sudden one day, it was gone?

There never could be any what-ifs! She knew who she was! She was Guida Santucci! She knew people's secrets, she earned a living!

She charged sixty-five dollars an hour for a seeing, but if you served her a meal, not a cheap little platter of Ritz crackers and pasteurized cheese from a tube, she'd put in an extra hour for free, deducting the time it took her to eat.

Her idea of personal luxury, besides a basic ability to pay her bills, was eating meals in other people's houses.

She knew everyone in the beleaguered, budget-slashed social service departments of the valley. The social workers, the few that were left, looked at her as a colleague, which had a lot to do with how she dressed. She was always seeing customers at two nursing homes and the three hospitals in the valley.

The regular hospital was lucrative because the turnover rate was consistent and the patients tended to have cash in their wallets to pay for things like TV rentals and getting their hair done, so she was often given big tips. The rehab hospital was tougher: there, her customers could be bitter and emotionally unpredictable, having been in car wrecks, all kinds of surgeries that got them nowhere, beatings, attacks, accidents, football games, soccer games, hockey games, war.

The county chronic-care hospital was her favorite because some of her customers there were in a coma; their families left an envelope of money for her with the nurses. She was picky about accepting bookings from the county prison for men, but it was only minimum-security, so if things were slow, she'd go out there.

There was no set pattern to the days of the week she went to work. One week she'd be off for three days in a row; the next, people would be calling every day. Six months could go by of never working on a Saturday, and then all she'd be doing was working Saturdays.

Money was like rain. One month, it could rain very often, buckets of it, and she'd make as much as two thousand dollars; and then the next might only be drizzly, and the next, sunny, with only three or four hundred, or zero.

The maximum number of seeings she could do in one day was five. But that was stretching it: five could only happen if her travel time from one to the other was minimal, which it rarely was. She'd done six, even seven, but only when she was very much younger, and only in institutions, where all she had to do to see her next customer was walk down the hall or take an elevator. Four was more like it for a maximum, but four in one day was rare.

For new customers who were not in the loop of social or correctional services, there were precautions, even if the customer knew Guida already.

If you wanted her, you would first have to know, or find, someone who was with her already. You would have to meet face to face with an old or current customer, who would have to be given your particulars, including your name, telephone, address, where you work, where your children, if you have them, go to school, and a credit card number, not that Guida took credit; she only took cash. New customers would also have to be willing to pay a fee of ten dollars directly to the person who referred them, like a tip to a waiter.

From the moment you started the process of inviting Guida for a house call, you'd have no direct contact with her in regards to your first appointment. If you were talking to her on her porch because you'd come to read her water meter, and she was going to your house next week for a seeing, you could talk about water meters and that was all. She'd go to your house the first time as impartially as if she were there to unclog your kitchen drain. She'd be a perfect stranger, it would seem, knowing nothing about you.

When Guida did a seeing, she brought no props, no equipment. She never used props or equipment like a good-for-nothing photographer who would pose you, flatter you, soothe you, and click away, and never mention that the camera had no film.

She brought only herself. If you offered her a cup of tea, she might drink it, but she did not look at leaves, either loose or out of a bag, like a show-offy, tea-reading cheat. After tea has been made, she felt, you should throw the leaves in the garbage.

If you held out your hand to her, she would shake it, not look at the lines of your palm like a palm-reading swindler. She'd ask only for a chair.

She did not make furniture shake. The chair was to sit on, a comfortable chair, and preferably, the chair would be a low one.

If she shut her eyes during a seeing, you should worry, because it meant she was falling asleep. She did not go into trances like ventriloquistic fakers who take your money and gloat like robbers for how they tricked you. If she fell asleep during a seeing, she didn't dream about customers. In fact, for all of her life, until the day she walked into the Hathaway and Tara was sitting there, she dreamed only for herself.

There was no crystal ball; there was no deck of cards. In her purse were no charts, folded up in neat squares, with pictures of the phases of the moon or the perambulations of the planets. She was not an astrologer. The astrological sciences, she felt, were like fairyland.

Never once in all the years of her professional life had she allowed a customer to bully her into acting the part of a fraudulent, so-called medium. There was only one thing to say about mediums. If you talk to people who are dead, they don't answer.

She had *standards*. She would look at a customer, and she would listen, and she would see how things were, and she would say, at the end of the seeing, "This is how things are." She would make a few guesses on things that lay ahead, but they were always based on tangible evidence. She never called them "predictions," but the general feeling in the valley was that when Guida Santucci made a statement about something in the future, it was probably going to happen.

"You are going to bankrupt your family and lose your home if you keep on going to the racetrack four times a week," she might say. Or, "The famous Hollywood movie star you wrote to eight times is never going to turn up at your door and ask you to marry him." Or, "You should not get your hopes up that the manager of your department, as evil as he is, will drop to the floor, dead, in the very near future, of natural causes."

But sometimes, if her mood was right, and if a certain type of feeling came her way—a certain kind of light-headed, sudden giddiness, like the instant before a sneeze—she would find herself gazing with her strong extra eye at something that no one else could see.

That was what was best: to see something and know that it was real, even though it wasn't an actual thing.

Sometimes it was simple. She'd be sitting in a chair in front of a customer who was forty years old, who'd be talking about problems with a bank, or a mother, or an alcoholic husband or a child in trouble at school, and there'd appear, like a photo in an album at the backs of her eyes, an image of the customer at the age of ten or twenty, doing something very specific, like dangling from a tree branch, or assuming a pose of a student in a judo class, wearing the appropriate jacket. There'd be no indication that the customer had ever climbed trees or learned judo.

She'd say, "Without fear, just for the thrill of it, you hung like a monkey from trees when you were a girl." Or, "Go back to your lessons in martial arts." And the customer would be amazed. Sometimes, Guida was amazed herself.

Sometimes it was a little more complicated. Once, in a seeing for a man named Charles Mahoney, who ran a chain of car washes, Guida saw a sharp, perfectly-defined image of a freckle-faced, seven- or eight-year-old boy with thick, bright yellow hair, and he was crying.

He wasn't Charles Mahoney. Charles Mahoney had dyed his hair as black as ink to hide the gray. She'd known him as a child; he was never a blond. The image Guida saw looked just like Dennis the Menace from the comics, for some reason sobbing his heart out. Why should Dennis the Menace be in her eye? She didn't mention it. She thought, "It must have been some kind of malfunction," even though nothing like it had ever happened before.

Three days later, she got a call from Charles Mahoney for another visit, right away. He had tried to convince her the first time that he'd only wanted some tips on his general future, but the truth came out. He'd been trying to decide if he should take out an ad in the county paper's personals. He was divorced, and it was driving him crazy to be alone. He wanted Guida to help him think of what to say in the ad, and he also wanted her to screen any answers for him and pick out the best possible choices, as if those were things Guida would do.

Again came Dennis the Menace, again in tears, and Guida heard herself say, "Don't place an ad, Charles. Answer one that's already there."

Could he do that? Oh, sure, he had the ads right there. He put the newspaper in Guida's hand, and it wasn't as if she simply put her finger on one particular spot in the columns under "Women Seeking Men." She read them carefully, each one, and at the end of the seeing, she took off her glasses and pointed to an ad that said, "Thirty-eight-year-old prof. seeking nights on the town, maybe more, with a guy who's worth the price of a babysitter."

"But Signora," Charles Mahoney protested, "I have six kids, I don't want a new wife with any kids. I want to go on cruises to the Bahamas. I want to walk around a lady's house in my underwear."

"Call her," said Guida, and he did. His hand was on the phone as she was leaving. He hadn't tipped her, which he could have, he was loaded, but the second seeing had only taken twenty minutes.

She never heard from him again, but she took his silence as a positive sign. If she had picked the wrong ad, he would have wanted his money back, or another seeing for free.

A little over a year went by, and one day she saw Charles Mahoney in line at the movies on a Saturday afternoon and he was holding the hand of a child who was too young to be his own. It wasn't a boy, but Guida was never fussy about details. The girl holding Charlie's hand was seven or eight, and she was a little bit pudgy, and a little bit overly round. She was wearing denim overalls. Under the overalls was a striped short-sleeved shirt, exactly like the shirt of Dennis the Menace. Guida was too far away to see if the girl was crying, but she probably was. The film they were waiting for was *The Lion King*. The line was very long, and the girl and Charles were near the end. She was probably crying because she was afraid she wouldn't get in. Her hair was bright, bright yellow. Her skin was the type of skin that would freckle.

Guida had an impulse to wave to the girl like someone she knew, but she didn't. She just stuffed her hands in the pockets of her coat instead.

All along, when she'd told Charles Mahoney to answer an ad instead of placing one, she was only thinking about whether or not he would pay her for the second visit, for failing to do what he wanted. She had thought she was taking the easy way out.

That was the only time she wondered if malfunctions could occur with her eye. It had never been one of her fears.

What if? What if? What if all of a sudden, it stopped working? What if all of a sudden, it was gone?

"But I am Guida Santucci," she said to herself. "I know who I am, I am Guida."

Gone! Gone! She could not believe she had not seen the fire coming. When she stood in the road at the bottom of White Cliffs

THE WHITE PALAZZO

Hill, and looked up, she felt her age as she had never felt it before. She felt as if a sack had been placed on her back, full of bricks.

A man went by on a bicycle. It was Dennis Chancy, who ran the dry cleaners. He slowed down and called out, as if she'd climb on his handlebars, "Signora, the fire's over, you want a ride home?"

She saw Dennis Chancy in his store almost weekly but she looked at him as if she'd never seen him before. He smiled at her and looked worried. "Signora, your coat is buttoned all wrong."

Guida looked down at herself. She'd thrown on her old winter coat, on top of her nightgown. It was as crooked as if a two-year-old child had done the buttons. She still had her hands in her pockets. There was nothing she could do about this problem.

The hem of her nightgown had dragged in the road and it hung below the coat all dusty and tattered, but she couldn't do anything about that, either. When Dennis Chancy drove away from White Cliffs he rang his bell, and it tinkled in the air like something breaking.

She could not shake the feeling of being dazed, as if hit on the side of the head with something heavy. She even patted herself, feeling for a bruise or a soft spot. Nothing was there; she hadn't been dented at all.

But sometime in the last week or so, she might have fallen or walked into a door, not that this was something that had ever happened to her. She was only trying to find a way to not leap to the conclusion that the worst of all possible things had taken place.

Maybe she had suffered an inexplicable, completely internal injury, and her brain could not recall it. The frying pan on a hook on the wall by her stove could have fallen somehow and smacked her and she'd hung it right back up. Last week when she was washing the floor of her bathroom, on her hands and knees, she might have misjudged where the sink was, and hit her head on it. It was a porcelain bowl, very heavy. She might have blacked out. Of course she wouldn't remember. Why should a brain recall its blows?

The firemen went away. There was a sense in the air of people sighing, as if they'd watched some holiday fireworks and now the smoke was trailing away and everyone was walking away and saying, "There, now that's over." The huddle of Gallaghers had come apart. There weren't black cars in the road with a hearse, waiting to take them away, but that was how it felt. The Gallaghers weren't wearing black clothes, but in Guida's eyes they were.

Soon it would rain in great sheets, she had felt. She thought she could feel rain coming, a hard, wash-everything-away, windy, rough rain, without thunder and lightning, just water. If the beautiful old willows that used to stand off the patio at the end of the White Cliffs back garden were still there, she predicted to herself, they would soon start tipping their leaves and curling up the edges, like streamers of light-green pods. If the grasses were there, they'd start bowing. "Sheets," she said to herself.

But she was wrong about that, too. It only got foggy. It didn't rain. She went home from the fire and locked the doors.

For five days she stayed put, shut up in her house as though she'd never go out again. The one time she turned on her television, it was tuned to the valley cable channel and they were talking about the fire, which wasn't fair. There was a bit of a video of the Gallagher family standing against the background of where White Cliffs used to be, and someone was saying, in that familiar, local-news-announcer way, "This former well-known landmark had a whole lot of history before spending some forty-odd years of being a classic New England restaurant and basically, being built originally around 1920, it's a safe bet to say that some of the electrical system was that old too."

She could have kicked herself for leaving her television on that channel. She only watched it because one of her customers was the weather reporter, and another was a very old man who watched the channel exclusively, all day long; it was the only thing he wanted to talk about.

On the screen were the Gallaghers. There were fewer of them than Guida remembered seeing.

Time had gone by between the morning after the fire and the day the Gallaghers were filmed. Over the Gallaghers' heads, there wasn't any gray-blackness; the smoke was cleared away. So they must have gone back up to the hill to pose for the cable camera.

Guida closed all the shades and kept them that way, except the one in the parlor that looked out on her backyard. The leaves came off the crabapple tree a little early this year, but there was still some green in those ugly little branches. The pears in the pear tree were ripe, with that yellowy glowing of autumn, and they were plopping to the ground for the lazy old crows to devour.

Only the young ones had the knack and the energy to peck at the pears in the tree. If you didn't look closely, you'd never notice that every pear in the yard was pocked through with beak-holes and bird-bites. Soon a rotty sort of heavy, fruity perfume would fill the air.

After the fire, she could have had as many appointments as she wanted, every day, and evenings as well. She could have been choosy about her bookings. Plenty of people wanted bookings. All they wanted to talk about was the fire.

"Signora, I'll make chicken cutlets with peppers how you like it, if you come over and see my Uncle Victor, he was the janitor up there, he's freaking out, because sometimes he was up there late and slept over, he's got a little room, and that night he was supposed to, but he got drunk and slept in his car, and he's walking around making everyone crazy, going, 'I could've been toast, I could've been toast.'"

"Signora, Fire Chief Ninsky says, will you go see the four guys in bed with inhalation, plus one also had a beam go almost on his head, and the Chief says, he'll give you a paycheck like an auxiliary, plus, he will make you beef stew to knock your socks off, if you tell them, seeing as the four of them just quit, and that is eighty percent of the department, guys, go back to work, nothing will ever be this bad again."

"Signora, come to my house as soon as you can. I got a sirloin in the freezer I was saving for my husband the assistant manager, but if you come, I'll defrost it just for you."

"My sister-in-law the banquet waitress? That lost her house last year from a fire? The one that won the checkoff, for how she makes her own ravioli? Will you please come? Please, Signora, she can't sleep."

Guida said no to everything, even to the aides in the nursing homes she was fond of: everyone was having terrible, lavish dreams of all sorts of fires, and the ones on the weird medications were having it rough. "Signora, we'll give you one hundred dollars and Chinese take-out, Peking duck, if you come for half an hour and calm down some really old people. Say the future's great and nothing else is burning."

When people came over, she stood in her doorway and shook her head and muttered like someone with a head cold. She pointed to her ears, trying to make it seem as if the thing she had lost was her hearing, not her eye. She had never let anyone know that everything she'd become had taken place because of White Cliffs. Who could she be, with it gone? What was she supposed to do instead?

The only reason Tara Barlow's parents got through to her was that they took her by surprise.

In the yard near the crabapple tree, poking up from the dry, yellowed grass, there was part of an old stone birdbath. The top was long gone: this was part of its pillar. It was two feet high but it seemed much larger, as ugly things always do: it was stained all over from crabapples, mildew, and droppings of crows.

The base of it had sunk in the ground just deeply enough so that, on her own, Guida couldn't pick it up and move it out of sight into the bushes. She had tried many times to hire someone to come over with a lever and pry it loose, but no one would. Everyone who ever looked at it would not believe that it was the bottom of a birdbath, as if Guida had her own private cemetery with one, small, partially ruined, decrepit grave.

It was just about twilight. She was on her way into the parlor to close the window shade and turn the lamp on.

She wasn't sure what had caught her attention. It was something in the yard, but it wasn't a movement. Nothing was moving. And it wasn't a sound. Everything was perfectly silent. "Something," she said to herself, "is out there by my stupid stone stump."

A white cloth, a long one, banner-like, was stretched across her yard. It was hanging like a bedsheet folded lengthwise, as if someone had draped it in half, almost perfectly evenly, on the rope of a clothesline. But there wasn't a clothesline in Guida's yard. What didn't go to the cleaners, she dried on a rack in her downstairs bathroom.

She ducked away from the window, went back to the edge, ducked away, went back, and did not turn the lights on. It occurred to her that whatever was wrong with her, it was getting worse, and she was seeing things that were not there.

Did blind people hallucinate, not that she was admitting she was, in a way, *blind?*

But there really was a bedsheet out there. What looked like a post or a pole at the other end of the yard, near the pear tree, was a man, a very tall one. This was Tara's father, Don Barlow. He was wearing a gray raincoat and he was holding one end of the sheet.

The other end was in the hands of Tara's mother, Adele, or Dell as everyone called her, and she was also in a gray raincoat. She was standing on top of the stump of the birdbath to be closer to her husband's abundant height. On flat ground she was only a little over five feet, and because she was obviously, even in a loose coat, very fit, very slim, she looked even shorter, like a grown-up version of a child gymnast. She'd climbed up on the stone to use it as a footstool. She held her feet tightly together at the edge, like someone getting ready to dive off a platform.

Don and Dell, like two bells.

The sheet in their hands was high enough off the ground so that the grass didn't touch it. It was no use trying to read their faces, except to notice that they were both very tired. Not once did either one of them glance over at the other to send a nod of support, or to see what the other one was doing, as Guida would expect in two people who did not trust each other very deeply. They seemed to have had a lot of experience, between them, of concentrating on something deeply, and of holding things up in the air.

It took Guida a while to realize that something was written on the sheet. It wasn't a design in the fabric or some embroidery; it wasn't the shadows. She never wore her glasses around the house, only when she was putting on seeings, so it took her even longer to realize what the words said. They were painted on the sheet in shiny, oily black paint, as black as tar, in careful, big block letters, as with a brush you would use for a wall.

SIGNORA!

YOU MUST LOOK FOR

OUR DAUGHTER!

WE CAN PAY!

Don and Dell looked ready to stand there all night, and maybe knock on Guida's door now and then to ask if they could please come inside and use her toilet.

She had to go out there and talk to them. As soon as it was dark, nothing about the sheet would seem normal, or even explicable, in any way. The words wouldn't look like words, but like bits of the night itself, and it would look as if the sheet were all tattered.

Lights of passing cars would light it up; someone was bound to notice it, especially if the wind blew suddenly. It would look as if it were floating, and the next day, Guida's neighbors would call each other on the phone, saying, "Of course she would have to have ghosts."

And having gone out there to talk to them, she found herself nodding her head: yes, she would take on the job. Yes, she would come to their house. Yes, she would put on a seeing for their missing girl.

She said yes because she could think of no reason to say no. It seemed to Guida that, if her life as a teller of people's fortunes were an airplane, and she was the pilot, she had switched it over to automatic.

In the next five weeks, would she regret it many times? Would she wish she'd had the strength of mind to ignore those parents? Oh yes.

Five

AAA Discounts!
We have cable!
Full service kitchenettes!
Come on in!

The Hathaway Motor Lodge looked just like every other motel that Guida had been to, and like every other inn, boarding house, hostel, and real estate office, all over Massachusetts, which had never heard of Tara Barlow. Had Guida been wrong in simply taking it for granted that Tara never would have left Massachusetts?

It would not have surprised her if she'd made a mistake in second-guessing Tara, considering the problem she'd been coping with since the morning of the White Cliffs fire. Tara would have lit out for California, they'd thought back in town. Or anywhere else that was different, or anywhere else that was far.

"She was in shock, like an accident victim," they'd told Guida. "She is out of her mind like someone who joined a cult, and she was not all that mature to begin with."

Guida drove into the Hathaway parking lot. She'd held no hope that this place would be the right one. She'd planned to visit everywhere, and at least have the satisfaction of being thorough. Anyway, it was only an instinct that made her think Tara had never left her home state, and what good were instincts, when facts kept overruling them?

Tara would not have gone to a city, either, Guida had felt, and she probably would have wanted to be somewhere near a river, as people from their valley always did, even if the rivers were polluted. And what about those hills? Wouldn't she have wanted hills?

There weren't any hills around the Hathaway and there wasn't a river nearby. The only other thing on Guida's mind as she walked into the Hathaway was that she wanted to ask at the desk for advice on somewhere to eat. She couldn't face one more meal at a Burger King or Wendy's or Pizza Hut.

The one restaurant she'd gone by that wasn't a fast-food place was closed down. It was a seafood-and-steak place, shabby-looking, abandoned, with the biggest sign on its roof she'd ever seen. She had slowed down to look at it because the wind was blowing hard. A cheeseburger and a lobster were pictured on the sign, and the whole thing rose up so steeply, it seemed that the wind might knock it over.

Guida had paused to see if the sign would fall, and felt disappointed when it didn't. The wind had stopped abruptly; the sign stayed in place. There wasn't any crashing or destruction in front of her eyes to dramatize the way she'd been feeling since the fire. If the sign had been cracked off its frame, if the wind blew it over and it fell to the ground and broke apart in a hundred bits, she would have felt a little less alone. She would have said, to the sign, "I know how you feel."

The Hathaway was in the middle of nowhere. Behind it stretched acres and acres of woods. There weren't any cars in the Hathaway parking lot; certainly there wasn't a red Mustang. Guida felt sure that all she'd do was walk in and tell the first person she saw that she was hungry and it soon would be lunchtime and where should she go?

Into the Hathaway trudged Guida, heavy-hearted and tired. Should she have done everything by telephone instead? She had held no faith in phone calls. What if Tara had checked in somewhere with a different name? What if she had bribed clerks to lie for her, or, if not bribed them, just asked them? Guida had wanted to find her with her own two eyes.

And there was Tara, alone in the Hathaway lobby, on a stool behind the counter, as if minding the desk for the owners, with the usual motel things nearby: an ice machine, a coffee machine, a pay phone.

And then everything changed in less time than it took Guida to blink, and to know that her eyes were not deceiving her.

It was Tara, all right. Guida had seen enough photos of her, and she had listened to enough descriptions, to know that the face Tara turned to her was fixed in her usual expression: a little bored, a little guarded, a little wary, a little impassive. She'd had a way of dulling her eyes for photos, even as a very small child.

Her eyes in real life were light and shiny. As astonished as she must have been to have looked up like that and suddenly, there was Guida, she hid it well.

Tara's family had never been customers of Guida's before, but many of Guida's customers were in the plastics factory, and lived in the Johnson Street blocks, and of course Tara would know anyway who she was. Everyone in their town knew everyone, in the normal small-town way, and when it came to Guida, everyone knew her especially.

Tara stood up when Guida walked in, and one second later, she sat down again, the way sociable, polite, tall people don't exploit the fact of their height, and never stay standing for long when they are talking to someone who only comes up to, more or less, the top of their rib cage.

Guida owned high heels and she was good at wearing them, but with the amount of ground she'd been covering, she was wearing her one pair of flats. In the flats, Guida was five feet and one-half of an inch.

As for Tara's hair, it was obviously the hair of someone who'd had a crewcut, and it wasn't so much growing as sprouting, like a head full of fuzzy, downy sprouts. They'd told Guida back in town that Tara shampooed with Clorox. Most of the white was gone but it still looked a little bleached: it was yellow and white, like silk on ears of corn, if half the silk is albino. She wore real clothes—corduroys and a sweater and Nikes and socks—and except for her hair, she looked like a normal person.

That was the first thing Guida said to her. "Oh, Tara Barlow, you look normal."

"Is that a compliment?"

"It is."

"Do I have to call you Signora like everyone else does?"

"You can call me by my name," said Guida. She liked the way Tara said "signora," clearly and easily, not at all like an American, and she managed to ignore it that the tone of Tara's voice was obnoxious. This was not the way people usually spoke to Signora Guida Santucci.

But she'd expected a little hostility. "Good at being hostile," was one of the things people had said about Tara. Some others were, "We'd never try to guess what she was thinking, because we'd always be wrong," and, "She has terrible, terrible manners," and, "She's good at holding grudges."

"Guida," said Tara, "have you got a new job, such as, now you're a detective?"

"Do you think I look like one?"

"No." Tara pointed to Guida's clothes. "You have a very nice outfit. If I met you on the street and had to put you in a job, I'd put you in a department store, a Republican one, very middle age, very traditional, possibly even extremely so, but not right-wing."

"I am not," said Guida, "Republican."

Tara pointed out the window to the parking lot. Only one car was out there. "You drive a Buick."

"It's a rental."

Guida's own car was a Toyota Celica and it was far from young, and it looked a lot older than it was. Back at home, it was sitting in her driveway, so it looked as if she'd never left her house.

Celica was a model that was rendered obsolete when Toyota started marketing Camrys. Tommy Ernst had a navy-blue Camry. Guida's car was also blue. She couldn't help it. She didn't know what came over her, but she just simply couldn't stand there and say, "I own a Toyota Celica."

"I own a truck," said Guida.

"I find that hard to imagine."

"It's black," said Guida.

"Well, if I had to find you a job, I'd put you somewhere like Bloomingdale's, where they really go in for pleated skirts and nice silky pearly-button blouses, and if you want to know which department, housewares. Or maybe ladies' accessories."

"I'm still just a basic, small-town psychic," said Guida. "Even though lately, it has not been going very well."

"But you found me."

"It would seem so," said Guida.

She watched Tara's face carefully. First, she had to get used to the fact that someone from home knew where she was, which she couldn't possibly be happy about. Then soon enough, she would have to work it out that no one knew where Guida was, either.

Guida was supposed to be working for the Barlows back in town, at home, looking for Tara while sitting in a chair with her eyeglasses on and her feet planted squarely on the floor, not in real life, franti-cally taking buses and taxis and renting cars and walking into motels and making phone calls, and spending she didn't know how much money, trying to buy news from gas station people, clerks, real estate agents, tollbooth attendants, the police, the people who work on road crews, the people who clean toilets at public rest stops.

"What kind of black truck?"

"It's a Ford pickup, one year old."

"Where is it?"

"It needed to stay home," said Guida. She was glad that Tara didn't ask her for particulars on a model. She wouldn't have been able to picture one specifically, now that the part of her brain that pictured things was gone.

When she tried to picture something, what was there? There was nothing in her mind but herself, trying to picture something. This had never happened to her before. She'd look for something in her mind, and she'd go blank. It had been this way since the fire; it felt like it would be this way forever.

"Did you leave this truck because someone else needed to use it?"

"There's no someone else," said Guida.

This was not the way they were supposed to be talking. They were supposed to be talking about home. Guida was supposed to be doing her job: she was supposed to be talking to Tara about the people she'd left behind.

The sounds of their voices were very much with her. She was not supposed to be ignoring them.

Tara's parents. "Find her. You must. We can't sleep."

Tommy Ernst. He had tried to wear sunglasses at work but they made him take them off. "I wondered if I'd have to start telling people my eyes are so red because I just started swimming every day in a pool and I'm allergic to chlorine, but everyone knows I can't swim."

The partners, like a chorus. "Find her so we can kill her."

Tommy, again. "As soon as you get in touch with her, tell her I've been talking to people at different restaurants and I've got it narrowed down to three and they're all very classy, very filet mignon."

A client of Tara's named Hector, who wouldn't tell Guida his last name: he was long-term temping at night at the desk of the Holiday Inn, and by day as a sorter at the post office. "Find her because I got eighteen people coming here next month from Brazil and they got to get work."

More Tommy. "Since the minute they called me and said she took off, I walk around like I'm walking around in poisoned air. She took the air."

A client named Sheryl Francese, eighteen years old, on welfare, with twin toddlers and an infant. Tara had fixed her up under the table as a receptionist in a computer company that had a day care center, but the company was switching to an automated answering service. "Find her so I can feed my kids. Find her so I don't do something nuts, like hold up a grocery store with like, a steak knife."

Tommy again. "I never believed in psychic bullcrap before but I swear to God I do now. Find her so the air can go back in the air."

A skinny twelve-year-old boy in Block Six on Johnson Street. "I always thought she'd be a rock star. Find her so I can go on tour with her like a roadie. I'm old enough."

Dan the security guard, stopping Guida by the door of the bank and putting both his big hands on Guida's shoulders. "If that girl does not come back, I am quitting this job. She was the only thing here that wasn't fuckingly, completely boring. I'll go back to washing Hondas."

And more Tommy. "I didn't even get my own note."

How many telephones were nearby? There was a phone on the counter, not three inches from Tara's hands, and the pay phone near the ice machine. Politely, discreetly, she could have waited for

Tara to gather her things and check out, although apparently, she'd have to check out to herself.

Guida looked at the phones at hand. She thought about the fact that motels have phones in every room, and there was nothing she could do about using them.

She did not know what to do. All she knew for sure was that suddenly, she would not have been any more capable of taking her eyes away from Tara Barlow than the needle of a compass could decide on its own not to point anymore to an N. It was the same as if many different things about Tara—her skin, the way she cocked her head to one side, the sullen line of her mouth, the height of her, the shininess of her—had conspired to form a grand, fixed point, which threw off some sort of magnetized *pull*.

She was nothing like the girl in the photos. She was nothing like everyone's descriptions.

It was the same as if there were no such thing as phones. Guida stood there and listened to what she wasn't saying to Tara. "Call your parents," she should have been saying.

Then, "Tommy Ernst is going crazy," and, "The partners want you to know that if you ever try to get work in another temporary employment agency, you will have to find one on another planet, as you'll never work on this one again. They would never write you a reference." And, "Tara Barlow, I've come here to bring you home to get married."

Was something wrong with her memory? No, nothing was wrong with her memory. She knew perfectly well what she was supposed to be doing and saying. It was the same as if a window had opened and a wind had come up, and all her plans and intentions flew out in little scraps, and she stood there, and did not run out after them.

Six

"They must have thought of using it when they saw what I took for a suitcase."

Guida had just told Tara about the sheet. Tara felt proud of her parents for getting through to Guida when everyone else had failed, but she wished they'd fixed themselves up before going to Guida's house, instead of throwing old coats on top of what they happened to be wearing.

"They must have thought of using the sheet because they knew that with me, it would work," said Guida.

"Did anyone think I was dead?"

"No one said so out loud."

"Did anyone *hope* so?"

"I wouldn't know what anyone hoped. I only know what I heard. But some people did, yes, very loudly and in public, very vigorously."

"That would be my four bosses."

"That would also be me," Guida said, "because the only place I'd have to look for you would be in morgues." The five weeks it took Guida to find Tara had felt like five years.

Tara hadn't made it easy. She'd done nothing wrong, so there wasn't any help to be had from the police, either state or any of the locals. She wasn't the victim of a kidnapping. She wasn't a runaway.

She had not applied for a job. The partners at Fillins found no word of her in their extensive connections with other employment agencies, or with their government friends and their tracking systems for things like social security numbers and taxes. Tara was officially nowhere.

The partners were no help and the bank was no help either. Of the four thousand dollars in Tara's checking account and the thirty-four thousand in her savings account, she'd drawn nothing. In fact, her checking account had grown in her absence, because the deposits she'd put down on those four valley houses had been refunded; Tommy had made sure of it.

She hadn't used an ATM. She hadn't written one check. Of her three credit cards, she hadn't used any, and she had not applied for new ones. She had some utilities stocks with a broker who had an office at the mall; she had not been in touch with the broker.

And there had not been one sign of Tara's car. She had missed her last premium but she hadn't canceled her insurance. Her loan was paid off, so Guida couldn't get help from the bank. It hadn't turned up in scrap heaps as a wreck, or on the side of the road somewhere, abandoned. The registration was valid; Tara had not applied for new plates. The Registries of Motor Vehicles everywhere didn't know where it was and neither did any police, state or local. Tara belonged to no clubs, although there were many clubs for Mustang owners. She was not the sort of person who joined things.

It was possible that the Mustang wasn't on the road at all: Guida had reported it as a stolen vehicle and there had been no word of it. Yes, she'd been willing to have Tara pulled over for driving her own car.

And Guida knew she hadn't sold it legally, either privately or to any of the, oh, many, many dealers she'd been in touch with.

Guida knew from the start that Tara hadn't gone north into winter. She hadn't taken anything to wear that was warm. When Guida had thought to break things down directionally, as in a compass, the one thing she had to work with was that there wasn't any north. She described all of this to Tara, calmly, in a business-like way—not the way she talked during seeings, but the way she talked to customers about fees and times of appointments.

"You went to my house? You knew what I took when I left? You reported my car? You wouldn't care if I was stopped by police and you looked at my clothes? You went into my *bedroom?* How much are they paying you, anyway?"

"I'm not supposed to be telling you this, but the one who's paying me is you. Your parents signed over your last paycheck to me."

"That was a whole month's check! Fillins only paid me once a month!"

"I already cashed it," Guida said. Quickly, she brought up the first of two questions that were most on her mind. "Are there any other guests in this motel?"

"It's not that popular of a place. Mostly it's only been the owners and me. They're out."

"Where's the Mustang?"

All this time, Tara was behind the Hathaway counter: if anyone had happened to pass by the lobby, it would have looked as if she were checking Guida in. But then she came out and around it. She didn't say "none of your business." She stood up, with every inch of her height going at Guida full-blast in the air.

"I was wondering how long it would take you to bring up my car," said Tara. "Come on. I'll show you."

Was there something about Tara's attitude that made Guida a little nervous? There was. Something alarming was in her eyes—hostility, yes; resentment, yes. If they were children playing a game of hide-and-seek, Tara was like the one found out, incredibly, in a place she'd thought was inviolate. She glared at

THE WHITE PALAZZO

Guida as if she'd raise her foot in the passion of a tantrum and kick her, or she'd leap at her and pull her hair, which of course she did not.

But it was not an option for Guida not to follow her, even though Guida was saying to herself, "Is she *up* to something?"

They went out into the sunlight, and suddenly something came into Guida's mind, sharply and clearly, as an actual picture, flashing at the backs of her eyes, where before there was nothing to see. It was that sign that had not been blown over in the wind.

That sign! *There* was something to cancel out the vagueness, the blanks. Colors! Neon red! A lobster in the midst of all those cows!

It only lasted a second, and at the same time, even as it was flashing, Guida felt that, if she and Tara that moment were magically transformed to the characters on the roof of that closed-down restaurant, the one who played the part of the burger, probably, would be her.

"It's not that far of a walk," Tara said. "We'll take the shortcut."

The rented Buick looked forlorn by itself in the parking lot, and Guida looked at it as if she had never seen it before. She followed Tara away from the parking lot, away from the rooms and doors of the motel in their u. Behind the motel, to the north, in the direction they headed, the trees appeared to have doubled in thickness in the half hour since Guida had arrived.

Some people have the ability to enter the woods confidently, without a telltale warning in their chest—a sort of fluttering—that comes on in a panicky way and means only one thing: the heart is in terrible danger. A heart, Guida felt, should just sit there and throb, not go moving around like a bird.

Some people like to stroll in the woods but she wasn't one of them, not even in the middle of the morning, with gold-white fall sunlight all around, caught and held everywhere—in the bronze leaves of oaks, in the green arms of pines, and in the air, and all over Tara's clothes, and on her face, and in her yellow-white hair.

Guida said, "This is a shortcut?"

"Don't tell me you're afraid of trees."

"I won't."

A packed-earth, well-traveled path was laid out through the woods, as flat and safe as a sidewalk, and Guida took the path and Tara did not. Tara ducked under branches and plowed through bushes, dead leaves, sticks, big roots, ferns as high as her knees, rocks, decrepit underbrush, mud.

To the east, through the trees where the forest was thinner, Guida could see a field with some apple trees—not an orchard, just three or four wild-looking trees. Wind was blowing lightly, and the rotty-ripe smell of the trees reminded her of home. There weren't any crows out here, cawing unseen in the branches. There were quiet, small brown sparrows, and higher up, some swallows.

Guida knew what the crows in her yard were doing. They were hopping around and sticking their beaks into the pears that fell from the pear tree and they were also screaming, because this was the time of year for selfish, excitable, hungry bees. The pears from Guida's tree were full of bees, and the bees were stinging the crows, and she wasn't there to hear them or help them.

The last thing she'd thought of when it came to Tara's car was that Tara would tell her she had buried it.

Seven

Woodview, it was called. It was enormous. It was the biggest cemetery Guida had ever seen. It was probably spread out over something like fifty-three acres. Fifty-three!

It was flat and treeless and green. If it weren't for the stones and flower pots, and stone crosses, stone angels, and many other monuments, and the narrow asphalt lanes that ran, like little avenues, between the long rows of graves, it would have looked like a golf course, but a golf course for very, very tall players.

A brightness was in the air. Even at this time of year, the grass was as green as if it came from an Easter basket: whoever took care of the grounds must have treated the grass with chemicals delivered from a tanker, like an oil delivery, and they probably said to themselves, "This is the one place in town where it doesn't matter that we're pumping the land full of poisons."

Meanwhile, Tara strode out of the woods well ahead of Guida, swinging her arms and looking not at all like a girl who grew up in a factory housing development, spending more of her time in her car than she'd ever spent on her feet. After what felt like a long time, she seemed to remember that someone was trailing behind her, someone slow, someone whose age was fifty-three. Someone *old*.

She looked over her shoulder at Guida to see if perhaps she hadn't made it through the woods in one piece.

Guida felt herself blushing when Tara looked at her the way she did, and it did her no good to wonder if she'd gotten a sunburn. Sunlight barely shone through those trees, and she'd only been in the forest five minutes. Guida liked how it felt when Tara looked at her and she didn't like the way it felt when she didn't.

"I am fifty-three years old," Guida said to herself, like a reminder. "Fifty-three!"

She looked around. There weren't any fences on the three sides that bordered the woods. The trees and undergrowth just simply stopped, and the grass simply rolled to its edges, like a carpet.

To the north, by the public road, there were high black iron gates, wide open. There was an ornamental arch above the gates, and in the arch was a scroll-like sign saying "Woodview," in tall, thin black letters, like letters that were formed out of fireplace pokers. The stone wall along the road must have been, a hundred years ago, part of someone's farm. But it wasn't falling apart. It was old but it wasn't crumbling. There were patches of young, firm cement among the rocks.

In all of Woodview, there wasn't a single black wreath or black banner. Many of the graves had a potted-plant, autumn-time floral arrangement of mums or geraniums. From the way the plants sat in their pots, and the way the pots were all wrapped the same, in green tinfoil, Guida guessed that they'd all come from the same florist. Up ahead, Tara waved her arm in the air, then again, then again. Guida wondered if perhaps she was waving at graves.

Then she noticed all the people. It had taken her a while to realize that in between the rows of graves, the cemetery lanes were full of people.

There wasn't a funeral going on. No one was on the grass. It wasn't unnaturally quiet, with a feel in the air of people who are forcing themselves to be hushed, but it wasn't noisy, either.

Guida had never seen so many sweatsuits in one place. Some people were strolling, and some were on rollerblades, and some were pushing baby carriages, and some were small children on bikes with training wheels, or those big plastic pedal-cars, and many were on all different kinds of bicycles, whizzing by with their heads and shoulders ducked low, or pumping their feet just enough to stay upright. Some people were jogging, and some were stumbling along as if they'd tried to jog and had failed, and some were just standing around, and there were also a couple of wheelchairs and one old man in many layers of clothes, pushing a shopping cart that was filled with empty bottles, clinking lightly. There were dogs being walked, many dogs. No one was on horseback, but Guida would not have been surprised if a horse had gone by.

When she caught up to Tara, Tara held out her hand and touched Guida's arm, just lightly, in passing. It seemed almost unconscious, as you'd pat an old dog you had given a command to, and half an hour later, the dog obeyed, not that Guida was thinking, "Well, I wish I was the dog of Tara Barlow." She liked the way it felt to have that hand on her arm and she didn't like the way it felt when Tara took it away.

Guida couldn't think of a way to say this, so she asked an appropriate question. This was the sort of valley that had elaborate, extremely attractive, state-funded bike paths.

Guida said, "Why are all these people in the cemetery? Why aren't they out on the bike paths?"

"No one goes on the bike paths except people who went to college."

"Well, I'm in the right place."

"So am I. It's better than everyone going walking at like, the mall. At least this way, people get to be outside."

Back in their town, people got into cars and drove to the mall when they wanted to go for a walk. Tara was right; this was better, as long as you didn't think about what was under the grass.

Tara pointed to the gates. "The car's this way."

The gravesite she led Guida to was the biggest one in Woodview. It could have held a small house. It was easy to make out the borders because there was a pole in each corner, four skinny poles, yes, like poles on a golf course, but instead of holding flags, they held yellow and black police tape, as if a crime had taken place. It was not like a crime scene in real life.

In a real-life crime scene there wouldn't be poles. That tape would not have been perfectly measured, and perfectly taut, and attached to the poles exactly in the middle and tied at the ends in *bows,* like shoelace bows, if the shoes were worn by giants.

There weren't any flowers at this grave, just grass. The stone was a simple granite square, unpolished. It was as long and wide as a sofa, and as high off the ground as Guida's shoulders. The name on the front was "Major." Under the word was an epitaph.

In comparing his life
to the lives of most others,
he lived it like his name.

On the back of the stone was a death date. Guida had to squint at it; the numbers were very small.

"Maybe you should put on your glasses."

"I don't need them."

"My bosses are completely vain about everything, and they're not even fifty yet, but they have to wear bifocals, the four of them, and so does my mother, so I'm used to middleaged people who can't read without glasses, in case you're thinking I'm not."

"I can read."

It was not an old grave. There were lines and indentations in the grass, showing where digging had happened recently. The date of the death was almost five weeks ago. It was two days after the White Cliffs fire.

Guida said, "You're supposed to be showing me your car."

"I am." Tara pointed at Guida's feet. "You're standing on it."

Guida looked down at the ground as if the antenna of a car would poke up, like another one of the poles, and the ground would give way, and suddenly she'd be standing on a shiny red roof.

Tara said, "There's a very, very good auto body shop in the next town, the best one I ever saw, and they could have done a great job with the dents, and they could have got the, you know, stains out, but I didn't have the heart."

She touched Guida's arm again, and held her hand there a little longer, on purpose this time, as if she felt sorry for Guida for being an ordinary person who had to have everything explained, very slowly, in just words.

"He was a horse," Tara said.

Guida couldn't tell what she meant by this "he." She couldn't tell if Tara was talking about the Mustang. "Are you talking about your car?"

"My car," Tara said, "was a girl."

"The horse was Major?"

"He was."

The yellow tape, those bows! "Don't tell me," said Guida, "Major was a police horse."

"He was."

"Don't tell me your car had something to do with why we're standing here, Tara," and Tara nodded.

"What stains?"

"Maybe you'd better sit down." Tara said this as if she'd reach behind the gravestone and find a comfortable armchair. Guida sat down on the grass and Tara did too.

When was the last time Guida Santucci sat down outdoors on the ground? She couldn't remember. Maybe it was never. What about her skirt? That skirt had cost her a hundred and twenty dollars. Would the grass leave a stain on the back, would the lawn-care chemicals? Would she get up and find her backside wet? Under the skirt, much worse, her slip could also be affected, and her pantyhose, and her underwear too, all of it damp, all of it carelessly stained.

The sunlight was hot on her face. She didn't care if it burned her, if her skin blushed as pink as a tongue.

Tara said, "Imagine a black horse. Everyone loved him, and everyone thought he was heroic, which he was, and everything he needed, food, carrots, sugar, horseshoes, a roof over his head that didn't leak, electric blankets in the winter, really expensive hay, someone to brush him every day, he had it all, he was rich when it came to comforts. But all his life, from the minute he wasn't a colt anymore, all he ever did was go to work. He was all by himself. Then one night, he gets out of the stable."

"Don't tell me there was a fire."

"There wasn't. One night when they thought they locked the stable door, they didn't."

"Major bolted?"

"Imagine," said Tara, "being every night of your life in a stable by yourself and all you did was wait for something to happen that was different."

"Different things go on in police work all the time."

"Not that kind of different. Imagine waiting your whole life for a door you're on the other side of to not be locked."

"But a horse couldn't plan ahead into the future."

"Imagine that this one could."

"But a horse couldn't hope."

"Imagine."

"But a horse couldn't figure it out that something might happen that had never happened before."

Patiently, as if speaking to one of her clients, saying, "This is how you fill out a tax form, this is how you handle a time card, this is how you look in the mirror before leaving your house for your job, this is how you smile when your boss walks by, even if your boss is a first-class shit," Tara said, "Just imagine."

Then she wanted to say something to Guida about her heart. She touched her hand to her chest in the gesture that goes with "The Pledge of Allegiance."

Then she said, "It was such a dark night and it was cloudy. Major wasn't heading for the Hathaway. He didn't even know them. But everyone says he was used to the parking lot being empty. He went down that road all the time on patrol. There was never any red Mustang before in the Hathaway parking lot, so, to him, it was just like a big, flat, paved-over field. He wasn't watching where he was going, who would?"

Guida said, "How old was he?"

"Oh, you know, middleaged. But he had great eyes."

"Bolted," Guida said to herself.

"Maybe," said Tara, "if the moon was out that night, there would have been visibility. But there wasn't a moon. And the streetlight near the Hathaway wasn't working."

Because a door was not bolted, a horse had. "Bolted." What an excellent word!

"Bolted."

It was good for Guida to sit quietly and tip back her head to feel a little more of the sun, and say "bolted, bolted, bolted," as if this were the one thing that held her in place, anchor-like. Otherwise, when Tara, sitting beside her, not even two feet away, had flattened her hand and held it to her chest where her heart was, Guida might have given in to a great, unmistakable urge to fling herself nearer and do the same. What she wanted to do was put her hand on Tara's heart as if Tara wanted to say the "Pledge of Allegiance," and had no hands of her own.

"Light," Tara was saying. She was talking to Guida about light. "There wasn't one tiny spark of light, not even one little glimmer, and the lights from inside, and the lights from over the doors didn't reach in the parking lot, so, to Major, it was all just dark. Why should Major watch out for my car? This was the first time he was ever out at night by himself. He was just running. Then all of a sudden, he hit my car, and then he wasn't running anymore."

"Hit?" said Guida, and Tara nodded.

"Hard," said Tara. "Very, very hard."

Tears were in Guida's eyes and Tara liked the way she didn't brush them away; she let them sit there.

Once, Tara put a man, aged fifty, as an end-of-year temp-salesman at the Honda place. He was mentally balanced in every way except one. He said to Tara, "You look just like *Breakfast at Tiffany's.*"

She answered, "We've got the same neck, but I'm blonde, and I'm taller than Audrey Hepburn, even if Audrey Hepburn was in heels and I was barefoot," and he said, with a mournful look, "It breaks my heart when beautiful dark-haired girls all wish they were blondes. Did Audrey wish she was Marilyn? She did not!"

He gave Tara a pep talk about not having envy for blonde hair, when she was standing in front of him with blonde hair. Why couldn't he see a girl with blonde hair? Who could know? He must have had a reason to want to eliminate blonde hair. Tara had to get him into the dealer for his interview so she made him a promise.

She pretended to be a brunette, and said, "I promise you I'll never wish I was Marilyn Monroe."

Tara explained all of this to Guida. She felt that the only reason she brought it up was to make the point that sometimes, people don't see what's right in front of their eyes, their real, two eyes. She wasn't just trying to give Guida the chance to say, "Except for the fact you are a blonde, you really do look like Audrey Hepburn."

"I only told you about the Audrey Hepburn guy," said Tara, "to cheer you up, and secondly, to make the point that sometimes something is right in front of your eyes, but you see something different, which I happen to think is not that healthy of a way to live your life."

"Seeing what's right in front of me is not what I've been having some trouble with."

"Then what do you think of those trucks?"

Guida turned around. By now it was well into lunchtime, and a canteen truck was coming into the cemetery through the gate, with an ice cream truck just behind it. They parked one behind the other in the cul-de-sac where hearses and limos, on other days, had some turnaround room, as the lanes were all so narrow.

The ice cream truck had a horn that sounded like something a clown in a circus would blow. Through a loudspeaker on the roof, it played a clear, big-brass recording of "The Itsy Bitsy Spider." But this was the cemetery, so out of respect, the driver blew the horn and played the song only once. The canteen truck wasn't refrigerated but they made their sandwiches fresh every morning (they said). They had coolers with ice for their sodas. It was the same truck that went around on weekdays to the plants along the river: the electric plant, a ceramics factory, a cement-and-gravel foundry, and a mill that made corrugated cartons for the packing departments of other mills.

There were many, many people in those places who were willing to pay money for someone to find them something different from what they had. It didn't have to be better. It only had to be different.

Already, in the last four weeks, Tara had found different jobs, either temping or permanently, for fifty-seven people, even though, being new at it, she still just mostly moved people from one of the riverside places to another. Her fee was ten percent of your first week's paycheck, cash only.

But Guida didn't know about this yet. "Let's eat," said Tara.

"You want me to eat off a truck?"

"It's totally sanitary."

"You want me to eat in a *cemetery?*"

"Picture it as a park."

"In a park, the bodies are alive."

"Well, picture it as a picnic."

"For a picnic you bring your own food."

"Picture that it's a picnic no one planned. Picture it as a situation you just have to adapt to."

Once, in Tara's second month as a Fillins full-timer, the partners gave her a client named Bert Haemer. They'd given up on him and they wanted to see what she could do. She always thought about Bert whenever the subject came up of adapting to something. It was automatic. It wasn't as if she were thinking, "Bert Haemer was incredibly middleaged, and the girl who fell in love with him was even younger than me."

Bert Haemer was a fantastic, totally professional CPA, but he had a few problems with talking to people. He was stuck in the plastics factory doing inventories. Never once on his own had he found the right way to just do things the way he wanted.

Bert Haemer was perfect for a temp because temps don't have

THE WHITE PALAZZO

to talk, but he never could make it through the interview part of getting hired. He had a rough voice, very gravelly, and he'd spit out words too fast, like shot coming out of a shotgun.

Tara got him interviews at two insurance companies, the electric company, the bank, and Sears, and he blew every one.

He couldn't give answers to questions. She prepped him, she even went to interviews with him and sat in the hall. He was fifty-five. He didn't have a family, he had no friends, he lived alone. "Give up on him, Tara," said the partners. At the time, she was only nineteen. She didn't know that "giving up" was a possibility that exists in life like a fork in a road you can suddenly turn off from.

She didn't give up on Bert Haemer. Then one day they were talking in her office and he said, "Tara, I wish that, when you have to talk to someone who, you're sitting there, and you're not real sure how to talk to them, life could be like *Jeopardy,* and then I'd feel a whole lot better."

"Like on TV?"

He brightened up for the first time. "The one where they give you the answers and you have to figure out the questions."

Bert Haemer was not that strange of a man. Tara could see that he was telling her something important. She didn't feel she was too young to have someone's future in her hands, even if the someone was much, much older.

Bert Haemer wanted to be the one who asked the questions. It wasn't that hard to put aspects of *Jeopardy* into his future.

Just because it never occurred to an interviewer to run an interview like a game show was no reason not to do it. On Bert Haemer's Standard Fillins Client Profile Form, the line that asked for "hobbies and personal interests" was blank. Tara couldn't just put, "watches television game shows," so she wrote, "training for *Jeopardy* as a contestant, and feels that, if he ever gets on, he will win." She didn't show Bert what she'd put there. Interviewers always looked at the hobbies line. Tara sent him to a government jobs fair at the Holiday Inn with lots of copies of the form, all in sealed envelopes that said on the front "To Be Opened Only By Interviewer." This was not the way Fillins sent out clients. Tara only did it that way once.

Bert handed the envelopes out. It took him almost a whole afternoon. Finally, at the IRS booth, a girl taking applications said, "I always tape it! I watch it all the time! I love *Jeopardy!*"

The IRS girl had the predilection to do something a different way. It was all right that Bert didn't know what she was talking about. His ears picked up on *Jeopardy*. She did his screening in the booth and it came natural to her to let Bert do the questions, even though she'd never done it like that before. She described the qualifications for the job like this: "Must be a lover of detail, very fastidious about details, very careful, and very single-minded about the purpose at hand."

Bert asked her, "What is the perfect description of myself as a lover?" He did great. It was tax-return time anyway, so he started the next day. He went permanent in a week, and then the girl married him, and she was *twenty*. And afterward, he never had problems with talking.

You have to be willing to adapt to certain situations, Tara felt. You just had to be willing in a personal way to think of doing things differently from the ways you had done them before.

"Everyone doesn't have to do things the way they always used to do them before." Tara was just about ready to lean down to Guida, take hold of her by both hands, pull her up to her feet, and walk her over to where a line was forming at the canteen truck.

But just then, just as Tara leaned down, just as she was holding out her hands, and just as Guida was saying, "Aren't there any restaurants around here," what should come by in the lane, all shiny, all proud of itself, with its engine thrumming lightly?

"My *car*," said Tara.

She wished that her hands could have made it in time to Guida's eyes, to cover them like a blindfold. That sign shop!

They'd made her leave her car at the sign shop the day before and she wasn't supposed to have it back until Monday. She didn't think it was strange for them to want a whole weekend to add one more letter to a sign. How was she supposed to know that, not only would they be early with it, they'd decide to deliver it; they'd come looking for her? How was she supposed to know that, come Monday, Guida would still be with her? Guida's voice was like the voice of someone who's just been punched, very hard, in the belly, and then goes ahead anyway and speaks. "Tara? What am I really on top of?"

Tara wished that Guida would reveal herself as a person with a good sense of humor. She wished for Guida to throw back her head and laugh, horse-like.

Tara said, "All you're on is just Major."

"I see," said Guida, quietly. "How did Major die?"

"He had a heart attack."

"Was he a horse?"

"He was the head of the vfw, and he was decorated heavily, very heavily," said Tara, "in the second world war. He didn't have a family. He had an awful lot of money when he died and it was all for his grave."

"Did he have anything to do with any horses?"

"He owned them. He leased them."

"To the police?"

"Yes."

"How many horses are in the stable?"

"They're practically Mounties out here. Fifteen, I think."

Tara's eyes kept going from Guida's face, which was hard to look at, to her car, which was easy. She wished Guida didn't get up to her feet with her face all slack and her mouth hanging open. She wished that Guida didn't look dizzy, that she didn't look like she'd been hit.

She wished that she'd told Guida about her new career. She wished she'd shown Guida the pillowcase from home that used to be her suitcase—how it was now filled with cash. But how could she have done that? It wasn't as if, when Guida walked into the lobby, Tara could have talked right away about her advertising, saying, "Come see my sack of money." The last thing she'd wanted to do with Guida when Guida walked in was tell the truth. Why should Guida, who never should have found her, have the right to be told the truth about *anything*?

She felt miserable. What had she been thinking, why did she have to be so impulsive? Why couldn't she be the kind of person who thinks something out, who doesn't rush around following instincts? "I will change," she said to herself, as if she really did mean it. "I will completely reconstruct my whole personality and become a good person."

She wished she could go back to the lobby of the Hathaway and have Guida walk in all over again. She wished she hadn't thought of pulling a joke on her. Was that what it was, a joke? It had simply popped into her head to bring Guida to Major's grave, and the rest had simply presented itself.

She hadn't thought it would go so far. She realized she must have expected Guida to see through the ground and know that she was pulling her leg. Some psychic! But this was not a good time to say, "I was just pulling your leg."

Guida couldn't see through the ground!

She wished Guida hadn't turned her back on her and walked away, fast. Tara had to run hard to catch up to her. She wished that

THE WHITE PALAZZO

Guida could appreciate the fact that, back in town, when she was reporting Tara's car as stolen, Tara was having her name put on it.

And she wished that, when the Mustang cruised up to Major's grave, Guida had said something positive, such as, "Nice electronics, Tara," or, "I love how the colors stand out." The mistake they'd made in her name the first time around was fixed.

Tara wished it hadn't happened that the first thing she did to Guida's heart was make her feel that the only thing she could do with it was hurt it.

It took Tara a minute to go after Guida because she couldn't *not* check her sign. They'd left off the "w" in Barlow the first time around. She drove it like that all month, "Tara Barlo," waiting for the sign people to slot her in for a correction. She couldn't hold a grievance with them because she hadn't spelled out her name when she talked to them about her order. The sign shop people were Italian and what would they care about a "w"? Does Italian have a "w"? It does not.

She wasn't about to change how she spelled her last name, and she wasn't happy about driving around with that mistake, but the wait had been worth it.

Wanting the sign in the first place had been an impulse that really paid off.

It was a great sign shop. What she'd wanted was neon, but they'd told her it couldn't be done: neon, they'd explained, is not a portable thing. What they gave her instead of neon was a sign like an electronic scoreboard, but much more personalized and interesting. They really knew their way around electronic colors and light. It was as if they'd left off Tara's "w" on purpose, while waiting for inspiration for how to handle it.

Guida rushed away from Tara, not toward the woods, and not toward the trucks and the gate, but straight for the stone wall, as if she'd leap over it, then run down the road as if her clothes were on fire. Tara realized that she ought to go after her, and she meant to, but first, here was the Mustang, and it was perfect.

TARA BARLOW

FINDER

ALL CAREERS!

ALL JOBS!

ALL AGES!

She could have bought a roof rack and settled for a detachable sign, and just tied it on, and took it off, whenever she wanted. The sign shop people had felt that they could manage to get it attached to the roof from the inside, so it would look like the words were rooted into the body.

And that was how they looked. If you ignored the framework, which was lightweight and almost invisible, the sign on the roof was completely, absolutely natural, as if, unlike every other Mustang in the world, this one had grown antlers, but antlers of words, in silver, in red, in white, and in green. And they weren't charging extra for what they ended up doing with the "w." You couldn't tell that it was added on later.

Silver, white, red, green. Except for Tara's first name, the letters were in alternating colors. The "Tara" at the top was all silver. Then on it went. The "B" of "Barlow" was white, the "a" was red, the "r" was green, the "l" was silver, the "o" was white, the new "w" was red. The color slid out of the wonderful new "w" like water going down a drain.

The teenage boy who was making the delivery was ecstatic, and Tara didn't care that for the first time ever someone else was driving her car. "Tara! Tara! Tara!" he cried. "Check it out!"

THE WHITE PALAZZO

When the color finished draining from the "w" it blinked back on in such a sharp clear way, it looked as if the green were many shades brighter than it was. It drained out, blinked back on, drained out, blinked back on. It really caught the eye, it really glowed, like a new, different, green version of "Rudolph the Red-Nosed Reindeer."

Guida! Guida was all the way to the wall when Tara finally caught up with her. She looked ready to climb over the wall to the road, in her skirt, and Tara rushed over to her and took hold of her by the arm.

"Seeing how my car's here, please please please, can I give you a ride?"

"The last thing I want to do with your car," said Guida, "is get into it."

"I'm sorry."

"Did you think it was funny?"

Tara shook her head very solemnly. "Absolutely not."

"But you made up a whole story."

Tara looked at the ground. She felt about four years old.

The teenager couldn't blow the horn because no one blew horns in the cemetery, so he leaned out the window and called, again, "Tara! Tara! Tara!" He'd driven over to the lane that was nearest the wall. He wanted Tara to know that he was there to deliver her sign, not sit around like a limo driver.

"Take it back!" cried Tara. "I'll pick it up later! Today I want to walk!"

"You're kidding," said the teenager. It was unbelievable to someone who lived in the country that a sane person would pass up the chance to be on wheels.

After he drove away, Tara stood there, waiting to see if Guida would forgive her, which felt like looking at a cloud that hides the sun. She'd never felt like this before. What if the cloud stayed put? What if it darkened?

Guida stared at the stones of the wall, as if she were counting them. Was she doing arithmetic? Was she counting ahead, into the future, the number of times she might find herself in the unfair position of trying to decide to forgive Tara Barlow for something awful she had done to her heart (not on purpose)? Something stupid, careless, and irrational?

Or never mind the future, what about the next five minutes?

She wished she could send a message to Guida telepathically. "Zero," thought Tara. "The number of times you will need to forgive me, ever again, for as long as you know me, even if it's only five minutes, will be totally, absolutely, zero."

At last, Guida tipped back her head and looked at Tara directly. "I am not walking back through those woods."

"We can take the road," said Tara. She felt seized with a burst of shyness, as if the sun had really just come out, and was burning her. Then she said the next thing that came into her head. "You didn't say you thought I look like Audrey Hepburn, but blonde, when I told you how the guy who temped at the Honda place said I did."

And Guida said, "That's because Audrey Hepburn wasn't beautiful."

Eight

It felt very good to be walking. Everything smelled like autumn. They walked by maples that were completely yellowy-red, every leaf.

Guida said, "Look, there's a restaurant up ahead."

"Please don't say that word. I'm not eating anywhere where, that's what you have to call it, and if you have to ask me why, don't, because I don't want to talk about it, and don't say the 'f' word either."

Guida mouthed the word "fire" but did not say it out loud. Tara said, "Anyway the food in that place is supposed to be terrible. Aren't you Italian?"

"Italian *American*," said Guida.

"Well, still, you would be insulted by how they cook spaghetti in that place, not that I ever went in there."

On a narrow, twisty, blind-curve country lane, with only about one inch of turf before the woods start, you're supposed to walk single file, but they didn't. They walked side by side, with Tara sticking out in the road. She wouldn't have cared if trucks went shooting by, or if tractors came up from behind and tried plowing her down. If she walked in front of Guida, it would have been necessary for her to walk backward, as if a hole would open up in the ground like a crevasse, and Guida would slip and go down it.

Once, Tara put a woman, retired from selling Domestics at Sears, in a Christmas-temp job at the mall, in the ski shop. The woman wanted to temp because it was the first Christmas in her life she'd be alone. She'd only been a widow a few months. Her husband had been Italian American and he had served in the Army Ski Patrol in World War II. He'd been stationed in the Alps. He had told his wife that the Germans knew where the crevasses were: they were using them to save money on bullets. Her name was Mrs. Charles Innamorati. She never called herself anything else.

She was Italian American too, and she had talked to Tara about crevasses. She'd told Tara what it was like for her husband to be someone who was not found by Germans and pushed down one. Instead, after the Germans went back to their camps, he had to sit on the mountain quietly, sometimes by himself, listening to the voices of people who were down there, for as long as it would take before they stopped talking.

There was oxygen in crevasses. There was water. It could take a long time. Mrs. Charles Innamorati liked the ski shop because all the kids wanted snowboards.

Snowboards, she'd said, were safe against crevasses, which did not make sense. Perhaps she appreciated the extra width, who knew why? She had hearing aids in both ears. They were old and they were always going static. She liked the static. It was the only thing that muffled, sometimes, what she was hearing from the Alps, even though she was never there.

When you're trapped in a crevasse your body heat keeps melting the ice. It's a basic law of nature that you'd keep slipping down the fissure, inside the mountain, a little more. Many of the voices were weak, so she couldn't always tell if they were voices, or if all she could hear was falling snow. Many of the people who were pushed in the crevasses were Italians.

Mrs. Innamorati only started listening to these kinds of things when her husband died. She picked up where he left off. Tara knew she would never forget her. "I am someone," she'd told Tara, "who knows how to listen to snow."

Tara couldn't walk in the road behind Guida because she needed to watch out for crevasses. What would it be like if a hole opened up in the ground, Guida fell into it, and Tara could never get her out?

Why was she thinking this way? She had never thought this way before. It just seemed to come to her to have panicky feelings about never seeing Guida again, in spite of the fact that only a couple of hours had gone by from the moment Guida had found her.

It must have started in earnest when she stopped Guida from climbing over the cemetery wall. It must have started like some sort of internal mechanism which had clicked on, and she hadn't known it was there: some built-in emotional capability, which might be, she reasoned, completely pathological. But that didn't stop her from *liking* it. She liked the way it felt to have her heart move funny in her chest because she didn't want someone to vanish and never come back. Had she felt this way before, and just couldn't remember it?

No, she had not; this was really brand-new, but it reminded her of the first winter she'd had the Mustang. Who would think a Mustang could handle ice and snow like a car ten times its size, like a weighted-down pickup, or even better, like a tank?

But it had. All right, she'd bought winter-traction tires that had cost two hundred dollars apiece, but still. The first time the Mustang was out on ice, it clicked into a whole different dimension of itself; an incredible capability was there, built-in. It was only just waiting to be tested. It didn't know that other Mustangs weren't like this. It loved ice and snow; it took hills in the middle of January like the locomotive in "The Little Engine That Could."

Already she missed her car, but she didn't regret sending it away.

She and Guida were fine in the road side by side. No one went by except people on their way to the bike path, who obeyed the speed laws, and waved to them, and people leaving the cemetery, who were too tired to wave or speed. Tara liked it that the top of her leg was pretty much level with Guida's hipbone. The top of Guida's head was exactly as high as the place on Tara between the top of her ribs and her shoulder.

"Guida?"

"What."

"Am I going to have to tell you again that I'm sorry or basically, was it already enough?"

"It was already enough."

"Thanks."

"You're welcome."

It wasn't that hard for Tara to adjust her stride so that she was keeping pace with Guida. Or maybe Guida had adjusted hers. Tara said, "When my parents hired you, did you put on a seeing about me?"

"I had to."

"What did you see?"

"If you really want to know," said Guida, "nothing."

"Did you see the fire?"

"In real life, or before?"

"Both."

Guida told her the truth. The total of what she saw before the fire was the total of nothing. The total of what she saw when the fire was over was the total of ashes and cinders.

"It seems to me," said Tara, "you might be having a classic middleaged crisis."

"I am not," said Guida, "in the middle of my age. Middle would mean I'll live to be a hundred and six, which I am not, let me tell you, planning to ever do."

"Well, it's not like you're, you know, elderly."

"I'm *not*."

"Obviously." The word hung there. "I mean, obviously, you've been having some trouble with your job."

"But I found you."

"That doesn't count," said Tara. "I think I know what you're saying. Once I was stuck at home because of having my wisdom teeth taken out, and I watched a *Bewitched* on cable. Samantha lost her powers. She walked around for almost a whole half hour being normal. She was supposed to clean her parlor and didn't know how to use a vacuum cleaner. OK, it's not a basis for a real comparison, because Samantha was only about twenty-five, and it was a television show, but still. She collapsed on her sofa and cried her eyes out because she thought she'd have to go through her life just like anyone else. I felt sorry for her and I burst out in tears."

"It's not the same thing in any way."

"Well, I was on drugs when I saw it."

Then Tara remembered something else. She had gate-crashed a motivational seminar put on at a computer company: she'd been looking for software temps. The man who was lecturing was an occupational psychologist and he was focusing on the topic of "loss." The seminar was about employees finding ways to get along with each other face to face, because everyone was talking to each other on their email, even when their desks were apart by not even five feet. When it came time for staff meetings, around a table, no one knew how to act.

Tara expected the lecturer to talk about the loss of people talking to each other, but no, he talked about the fact that a good way to have a conversation with your office mates was to ask them what they'd suffered, such as, from someone's death, or maybe they'd just found out they were adopted, or someone they lived with was having an affair, or it was money on the stock market that they'd lost, or their youth or their hair.

"It's not the same thing at all," Guida said.

Tara remembered that the lecturer had said there are two things in the world that everyone has in common. One, simplistically, is a birthday. And the other one is the weight on your back of what you have to walk around with, of what you've lost.

"No one can help it how old they are," Tara said. "And everyone's got a weight of what they've lost."

No, she hadn't recruited anyone that day. The mood at the end of the lecture was too depressing.

"I think I see a *diner*," Guida said.

She was right. The name of the diner was Fuller's. "That's Fuller's," Tara said.

Fuller's Diner. Arby's Roast Beef. The Crescent Cafe. Pizza Hut. Jeannie's Breakfast. Alice's Wraps and Smoothies. Diamond Pizza and Subs. Dunkin' Donuts. The Blue Tip Grille. The Happy Wok Take-out. The Danny Boy Lounge. The Last Locomotive Pub & Grille. These were some places to eat that did not mention "restaurant," not in their name, not in their window, and not on their menu.

Tara said, "I'm so hungry, I could." She'd been about to say "eat a horse," but she saw the expression on Guida's face, and caught herself in time.

Don't say "restaurant." Don't say "horse." And also, try hard to never say "fire."

"I could eat everything on the menu," said Tara.

They went in. Some things to order at Fuller's were real, roasted, portable-Thanksgiving turkey sandwiches, hot, with two layers of gravy-lathered turkey, and stuffing spread onto the bread—onion-and-nut stuffing, heavy on the butter, like peanut butter for grown-ups—and cranberry sauce, the sugary kind, spread onto the stuffing. And three-layer cheese-and-bacon melties where you didn't care if your lips got oily with the grease. Amazing burgers. Chicken pot pie that, if you ever ate one frozen, you will never eat one frozen again. Sides of fries so big, they have to serve them on platters. Onion rings so big, you could wear them as bracelets. Pumpkin or chocolate pecan pie, heated up. A fruit cup to start with so you can feel you are doing something healthy, even if it's fruit cocktail from a can.

"The burgers are stupendous here," said Tara.

"I think I'll stay away from burgers," said Guida. "I want the fried fish."

"I want everything," Tara said.

A waitress came and took their orders. Tara was glad there was no one in the diner she knew. She would not have been able to stand it if someone she knew started looking at her, personally, in a strange and curious way, as you'd stare at someone with a new hairdo or new glasses, but you can't quite place what's been changed; you just know that something was.

But it would have been nice, Tara felt, this first time she ate a meal with Guida, if suddenly, fantastically, when their food arrived—and they had ordered a great deal of food—the big, heavy, old-time diner table between them groaned with the weight and collapsed, like a table made of cardboard; or else it would simply, in a cloud of sawdust, completely disappear.

They would have to eat lunch off their laps. They'd press their knees together and make a much better table of their knees. Tara imagined this so strongly she could almost feel the woolly fabric of Guida's skirt against her own skin, as if her own legs were bare.

She didn't stop and wonder what was happening to her. She looked across the wide, wide table at Guida, and said, "People back home always said you had an extra eye. Tell me about your eye."

Guida held out her hands, as if the words to answer this question were floating in the air and she'd catch them. But nothing was in the air. Tara said, "You should start with how you got it."

"At White Cliffs," said Guida, and Tara's eyes opened wide.

"No way!"

And Guida leaned back in her chair and folded her hands on the table. "I was a girl," she began. "I was Italian, and I was Catholic, and I was fat. And one day, it was raining."

Nine

Guida knew as a child that there were blonde Italians with tall, slim bodies, light eyes, fair skin, and small noses, who could walk through town, through the Irish neighborhoods, without worry; but she wasn't that type of Italian.

She was two years old when she was brought to America. The Italian part of town was where she lived. She understood every word of Italian that ever went into her ears, but the only language she was allowed to speak, even at home, even if no one comprehended her, was English. She had no accent. She wore American clothes. But it was the same as if a brand was on her forehead saying, "Wop."

Everyone knew that everyone was against you if you were a dark-skinned, wide-eyed, sharp-nosed, wide-waisted Italian with black hair, as black as a crow. The only school in town for Catholics was Irish, so Guida went to the Irish school.

On the day when things were set in motion for her to find out about her extra eye, it was raining, and she was ten years old.

It was raining for the fifth day in a row. The priests had put a ban on outdoor play in snow and rain, even if every child had a raincoat, warm clothes, boots, a hat, a sweater. The feeling of the priests was that the nuns, and the children themselves, could not decide on their own which types of weather to stay indoors from. So they'd forbidden it all, as if Nature, with its wetness and windy, strong forces, was bad for everyone, not just Catholics.

In the fog and gray rain, the inside of the school was like frantic, buzzing bees inside a jar. The priests stayed away at times like this, but today they sent help. They sent the single-ladies luncheon group of the Ladies Auxiliary of the Knights of Columbus.

It was strange to hear high-heeled shoes in the hallways, and smell face powder and perfume in the classroom. Some of the Auxiliary ladies were cocky, and called the nuns by their masculine names, leaving off "Sister" and "Mary." The other children laughed out loud when they said things like, "I'll mind your class, Robert, while you go smoke a cigarette," and, "Kevin, you could use a martini."

Guida sat in the row near the back of the room. The number of friends she had in school was zero. The class was a large one. Her row was slanted to make room for extra desks. It swung out from the body of the class like its tail.

"Hello there! Do you understand English?"

Guida was so startled that someone had spoken to her, she didn't know what to do. She'd expected the ladies of the Auxiliary to pay attention to the girls whose giggles, the priests said, were like bubbles from the throats of Irish angels.

The normal boys had been sent to play ball in the auditorium: there weren't any boys in the classroom except a boy who was a cripple. He wasn't in Guida's class. Another nun had wheeled him in. He was sitting in a wheelchair on the other side of the room.

No one treated him cruelly. No one treated him in any particular way at all. His body was curled at his hips like the curl in the center of a pretzel. There were metal braces on his legs, with hinges at the knees. His head was tipped back. He moved his lips as if talking to himself, and some drool trickled down his chin and down his neck.

"Do you like to draw pictures?" The Auxiliary lady wore fresh red lipstick that had blotched on one of her teeth, but Guida

THE WHITE PALAZZO

decided to ignore this. She was of a vague age to Guida: she was somewhere between "after high school" and "old."

She went to the closet for some good, thick white paper, and two pencils. "What kind of picture should we make?"

"Oh, the rain, please."

The pencil she gave Guida was one of the new art pencils, wider in the tip and darker in the lead than the ordinary ones. The Auxiliary lady didn't know that only the nuns and some girls who sat near the front were allowed to use them. The fact that Guida was getting a good pencil was incredible. She imagined the shading she would do to get the sky just right, so it would look like it looked out the window: like clouds of ashes. The rain would be silvery-gray, like needles. The lady from the Auxiliary said, "Rain's complicated. Let's think of something else!"

"But that's what I thought of," said Guida.

"How about a nice house and some flowers? We'll say it's in the country your people are from. Where would that be?"

Was this a trick question?

As the Geography Sister said once, "Italy, the Axis land of Mussolini, is a boot." She was a young, pretty Sister, with fair Irish skin and reddish eyebrows, and she was loved by the children for her playful nature. The map of Europe was on the wall. The Sister had a pointer and she pointed to the boot, and slowly, heavily, she lifted one foot in the air. She peered around at the floor and opened her eyes very wide, as if a bug ran by and she was getting ready to step on it. The other children looked at her shoe, at the swing of the hem of her habit. They saw a bit of black underskirt and black wool stockings, and were secretly frightened and thrilled.

When she finally stomped down her foot, she cried, "Mama mia!" and everyone laughed. It really seemed like there'd be a flattened bug on the bottom of her shoe.

ELLEN COONEY   99 ⁓

Guida laughed too. She had to. Everyone was looking at her. But it wasn't clear to Guida what those gestures or words really meant.

"Are you from Italy? Or is it—don't tell me—let me guess! Puerto Rico! Should we draw a Puerto Rican hacienda?"

Guida just looked at her. The Auxiliary lady frowned. She was thinking. Then she said, gently, as if she felt sorry for Guida, "Maybe I was wrong to say 'house.' Should we get out the crayons? Should we draw a nice trailer-park trailer for you, a big bright trailer, in a big bright colorful park, with lots of other trailers just like it?"

All along, the crippled boy must have been watching. There could have been no other source of the words that were suddenly uttered. If an animal had started talking, it might have sounded like this; a phonograph record being played at low speed would have sounded this way, too. It might have been the sound of the crippled boy moaning loudly.

But he was talking. "Dr-dr-drah! Mih-mih-mih-meee! Heh heh heh! Drah me!"

The room went silent. The game of jacks in the corner stopped, with a tinkle of jacks on the floor. At the front of the room, another lady from the Auxiliary looked up sharply, as if she'd sucked on a lemon, and the four or five girls she'd been reading to jumped up from their seats and hurried behind her.

It seemed as if the crippled boy might spring from his wheelchair and do something terrible, like attack them. The nuns always said that when someone's deformed, it's a reminder from God that Old Mother Nature, unlike Himself, isn't perfect.

This was another thing Guida never understood. Nature looked pretty good to Guida. Nature just looked like itself.

"Draw me! Draw me!"

The lady put her hand in a protective way on Guida's shoulder. The boy's face was softer now. He was laughing. Guida could see it in his eyes. The next thing he said was a question. "What's the m-m-m-matter? D-d-d-don't you th-th-think I'm ha ha ha handsome?"

The lady from the Ladies Auxiliary grabbed Guida's pencil away from her. Why would she do that, on top of not letting Guida draw rain? She just grabbed it right out of her hand.

"Don't be bothering the girls, you."

A nun appeared in the doorway. It was the Sister who taught eighth grade, who often took it upon herself to give punishment to anyone at all, not just her own pupils, in the yard, halls, and cafeteria, instead of sending you to the Superior. The eighth grade Sister's form of punishment was this: she swung out her arm as if playing tennis, and applied her hand broadly to your back, in a quick combination of slapping and punching, just below the line of the shoulder blades. The children all jumped at the sound of her voice.

The eighth grade Sister went over to the boy. She took hold of the handles of his chair, gave it a tug. It didn't move. She reached down and undid the brakes.

Now the boy was not laughing. The fear that came into his eyes was a terrible thing to look at, but Guida did not look away. Then the wheelchair thudded against a desk, and someone from the Auxiliary called out, "Sister! Be careful" It was clear to Guida that she said this because she was worried about the nun, not the boy.

Guida didn't say to herself, "Now I will bite this Auxiliary lady on the wrist and get back my pencil." It just happened.

She opened her mouth as wide as it would go, and bit down as hard as she could. Her teeth went down to the lady's bones. Her pencil slipped out of the lady's hand, fell to the floor, and started rolling away. The lady cried, "Oh, oh, oh, oh, oh! This foreign girl just bit me!"

How could the eighth grade Sister have appeared again so quickly? She must have left the crippled boy in the hallway.

Guida was bending over and reaching for the pencil. She knew that the eighth grade Sister had come over to her by the sound of the rustle of her skirt.

There was nothing Guida could do to stop what was coming. Then here was the blow to her back, as strong as if the hand of the Sister weighed more than Guida's whole body.

The blow knocked her out of her chair. She started falling straight down, but when it was time to land on the floor, she kept going. The thought came to her that her breath might never come back to her.

Maybe the hollow she was tumbling into would have no bottom. She'd heard about the study of geology. She knew that everywhere on the earth there were ordinary surfaces that could suddenly give way, because upright tunnels, or chutes, ran down through the core of the world and out the other side: one day, she could happen on one and go down, like a rock, and she'd never be heard from again.

But then, to her own surprise, she was finished with falling. The hollow had a bottom, a very firm one, very strong.

She was standing beside the crippled boy. His chin was all wet. His body looked a little more twisted and he sat in the chair at a different angle, as if he'd been trying to roll over, but had nowhere to go. His hands were curled up in his lap as if he were wearing invisible mittens, without thumbs.

Somehow, Guida's feet were on the smooth wood floor of the hall and not the tiled floor of her classroom. Behind her was the school auditorium where the rest of the boys were playing ball: she heard them running and thudding each other, very closely. And there was the big formal portrait of the Pope in a big bronze frame, not the simple one on paper that hung in the classroom.

It was the hallway, all right. How did she get out there? She said to the boy, "I don't know how I got out here. I thought I was falling in a hole," and the boy said, "Hi!"

"If you want to know the truth," Guida said, "I stink at making pictures. But as long as I'm here, want me to promise you something *excellent?* I'm getting that nun with a curse."

The boy didn't stutter any longer, as if the hallway were a magic place. "Great idea! You know how to do curses?"

"I'm not old enough yet. But I know someone."

"Can you do a whole lot of them at once?"

"I don't know. I never did this before."

"Put a curse on everyone here but you and me!"

"I think one at a time would work better," said Guida, and the boy said, "Thanks!"

Back in the classroom, she was allowed to rest her head on her desk for five minutes, and when the blood was back in her face and her breath came back, she had to go down on her knees and say "I'm sorry" three times: to the eighth grade Sister, to the Auxiliary lady, and as a general announcement to everyone else. When the class wrote a thank-you letter—"Dear Auxiliary, That was such a nice visit!"—Guida was not allowed to add her name. For homework she had to write, five hundred times, "I will not bite like an animal."

Then, when it was time to say the prayers at the end of the day, she folded her hands and bowed her head like a good Catholic child, but she wasn't saying Catholic words.

She had made up her mind to stop being Catholic. She would have to find new words. She started picking the old words of prayers from her mind, like picking burrs off a sweater.

Everyone else said an "Act of Contrition," an "Our Father," and a "Glory Be," and Guida said, "The capital of Delaware is Dover. The Athens of America is Boston. Michelangelo was born in 1475. Capital letters are for names of people and places, the beginning of a sentence, and things that are very important. The four basic tools of humanity are: the lever, the wedge, the pulley, and the inclined plane."

She never saw the crippled boy again, although she looked for him. He must have come from one of the other valley towns. She heard later that he'd been transferred to a school somewhere else, for cripples.

But she never forgot what his face was like when his eyes were lit up with pleasure, and then, a moment later, when the light had gone out of his eyes. She hadn't been kidding about the curse.

After school, she ran errands for Coochie Mastromatteo.

Coochie lived in a hot little third-floor apartment in the shadows of the carpet mill on Cransy Lane. Sometimes when Guida thought about her, she seemed like a witch in a storybook. Guida would pat her own belly and swear to herself that she'd never be flabby when she was old, with the ruined-like shape of Coochie's old body.

Unlike the other tailors on the street, Coochie didn't have a sign in her window, and she never put displays of her work on her stoop or out on the sidewalk. She had customers whose clothes she'd looked after for years, but most of her income was from the army base in the next town. Soldiers came by in an olive-green car every month to deliver their bags of heavy mending: when the new ones came up to the apartment for the first time and stood sweating in the tiny kitchen, they seemed relieved, as if it fit their idea of things in general that Coochie was rough and fat and strange, and smelled like someone who splashed on perfume now and then, and never stripped down to take a bath.

Coochie knew everything about the business and affairs of everyone in the neighborhood, and especially of all the Italians, including things that took place in the past, and, people said, many things that had not yet happened.

She sat in an armchair by her heater. When she moved around, even a little, the fleshy upper parts of her arms would wiggle. She wore a housedress and thick white socks, like a man. The heater was an old gas box, and the flame burned low, in skittering blue sparks, along the grate.

The room smelled like sweat and perfume and linty fabric. Coochie had burned herself many times by dozing off in that chair. She had scars all over her shins, as well as burns on top of the scars, all in the shape of the grate-lines. Under the socks she wore strips of flannel that she soaked with Mennen Pink Baby Lotion. The bits of cloth were tied in place with strings, in knobby little clusters. Guida could see the knots in little bulges through the socks.

Guida wore her school uniform: a white blouse and blue jumper that was supposed to hang loosely, but it was a little too tight around her middle. The starched collar of the blouse dug into her neck and left red marks, as if her neck had been burned. Under the uniform, the buttons of the blouse were not all buttoned because they didn't all reach, but no one knew this.

Coochie looked at Guida's jumper. She grabbed for the hem, turned it over, and checked it. Guida hated sewing, but she'd learned to be careful with her clothes. It was the one thing, she felt, that made Coochie feel glad that she knew her.

"You always have to be careful how you tie off your knots," said Coochie, and Guida took a deep breath. She hoped the floor she was standing on would hold steady, and there'd be no such thing as dropping feet first, down through all of Coochie's building, then down and down, through a chute to who knew where. She had never asked for a curse before, and she had worked out no plan of how to go about it. If it weren't for the image at the back of her eyes of the crippled boy in the hallway, she never would have worked up the nerve.

But she could see him. There he was, exactly in the spot where the eighth grade Sister had parked him in the hallway. If Guida had carried a photo of him in her pocket, and was looking at it, he would not have been clearer to her; he would not have been any more real. His hands were curled up. His fingers were like fingers inside an invisible mitten.

Guida said to Coochie, "People say you have three eyes. Did you already know about your extra one when you were in school?"

"I never went to no school."

"How did you know you had one?"

"Oh, you know. You just know."

Coochie seemed pleased that Guida had brought up this subject. When she smiled at Guida, she showed her gums and teeth and tongue. The roughness of her everyday manner fell away like a scab.

"Everyone says you put curses on people," said Guida. "Is that what you do with your extra eye?"

"No," said Coochie. "You must not think so, not ever."

"Is having an extra eye and putting curses on people two different things?"

"They are."

"If I give you the name of someone for you to put a curse on, does it have to be her name she was born with, or just the name she has now?"

"Did she change her name like a married lady?"

"Like a nun," said Guida, and Coochie said quickly, "Italian?"

"Your curses only work on Italians?"

"For Italians, you have to put in more."

"She's Irish."

"Then you only have to tell me her nun name," said Coochie.

Guida told her the name of the saint the eighth grade Sister was named for, and also, the address of her school. "School Street," said Guida. She felt proud that Coochie didn't ask her what the nun had done to deserve cursing: obviously in Coochie's eyes, Guida was someone to be trusted with these types of judgments. She was curious, though, about the possible forms a curse could take. Probably they were divided into two different types.

The image of the boy at the back of her eyes had just shifted. Guida imagined the eighth grade Sister in his place, in a bigger wheelchair, and from her neck to her feet, her body in her habit was twisted, like a sponge. She looked like a sponge that had been loaded with water, and someone was wringing it dry. She looked very, very worried.

Guida said, "Are you putting a curse on that nun that doesn't show, or are you putting one on that will show?"

Coochie thought about that. "Which way do you want it?"

"So it doesn't show." Guida felt that, if the nun were magically turned into a cripple, it wouldn't stop her from being cruel: she'd just keep on tormenting children, from her wheelchair. A better curse would be one in which no one suffered but herself.

"Maybe she won't sleep so good at night," said Coochie. "Maybe she'll be waking up all night from dreams she never had before."

"They can't be good dreams," said Guida.

"Good dreams, you don't wake up from."

This sounded all right to Guida. Coochie said, "Go get my purse from the drawer. It's time you deliver some drapes to the nuns at the white palazzo. But you got to be careful, they're silk. You know what I'm talking about, the palazzo? You'd think nuns, they know sewing, but let me tell you, whatever they sew, it looks like someone sewed it who was blind. You don't have to get them to pay me like usual with regular people, because those nuns, they don't pay."

Guida had never seen the white palazzo but she'd heard of it and knew where it was: just outside town, on the top of a hill that had no name. The road had no name, either, because nothing else was out there except woods and the turn to the army base. Everyone simply called it "the road out of town to the base," or, "out where the Sables used to live." The white palazzo had been built by a family named Sable, as in "mink."

Coochie said, "Get up early tomorrow morning and get your uncle to drive you when he goes by."

Guida's uncle was a businessman who sold supplies to bars and small local shops. Around dawn every morning he drove past the palazzo on his way to the army base, where he filled up his trunk with liquor and cartons of cigarettes. The source of his supplies was the post exchange. "I'll do it," said Guida. She felt she could get away with another question. "Is your extra eye inside your head?"

Coochie looked away at the flames of the heater and waved her hands, as if trying to find an answer in the air. The flabby paunches of her upper arms rippled, like waves, but she did not come up with words. She held her hands together at her big, wide belly. Guida had seen pictures of curled-up unborn babies. That was where it was? In her belly? Like a baby?

"You don't have to give me any money for delivering the drapes to the palazzo," said Guida. "Because of being so nice to me about doing the curse."

"Fetch my purse." Coochie handed Guida a shiny, brand-new dollar bill. Guida put it in the pocket of her uniform. She felt very disappointed. She had hoped that Coochie would reveal her extra eye, as simply as someone rolling up a sleeve to show an elbow, or a tattoo, just to prove that it was an actual thing.

But early the next morning, as promised, she went out to the Sables' white palazzo.

The Sables used to own the savings bank. "The bank when it was with the Sables, it crashed in the Crash," was how Guida had

THE WHITE PALAZZO

heard it described. The family had left the valley. They'd made a gift of the estate to the diocese, but for several years, before the Grayfrocks came, there was an interlude of emptiness. Many of the rooms were closed off, and the best of the furnishings had been taken away to the diocese's vaults.

The Grayfrocks ran retreats for Catholic women and lived quietly. Unlike Guida's nuns at school, they weren't Irish. They were mysterious, and they were Spanish. Some of them came from South America and some came from places like Cuba, Mexico, and Puerto Rico. The founder of their order was from Spain, the land of haciendas. Maybe that was why they lived in the palazzo, which was something that the nuns at Guida's school had never stopped complaining about. Why should the diocese let those Spanish nuns live like queens, and never have to slave in a classroom, when they, the Irish, who spoke English and worked like dogs, were given a shabby house in the bad part of town, without one inch of land for a lawn or a garden? The nuns from Guida's school never went out to the palazzo to socialize with the Grayfrocks.

The Grayfrocks' clothes were simple: short veils and loose, shin-length, gray sleeveless dresses and roll-sleeve white blouses.

The estate was a run-down version of its former self, but the lawns were green and hilly, and curved up toward the house in long waves.

Guida arrived with the package of window drapes very early in the morning, before dawn. Her eyes were still squinty and heavy with sleepiness. Her uncle dropped her off at the gate, and would return in an hour to pick her up. He had rarely ever spoken to Guida at all, but perhaps, today, he felt sorry for her. She'd never seen a rich family's palazzo before.

She looked around at the lawns, and at the size of the house, and he said, "Those Sables might be rich, but they pull down their pants to take a shit just like everyone else, and don't forget it, or I'll pop you one between the eyes."

"They're gone, Uncle. Nuns from Spain live here now."

"Well, don't trust them. An Italian will look you in the eyes before sticking a knife in your belly, but a Spaniard will give it to you in the back, and run away like a coward."

"What about the Irish?"

"The Irish," said Guida's uncle, "will come to you with one hand out and the other behind their back, with a brick. While you're shaking their hand, they will smash the brick onto your head."

"I'll be careful," said Guida, and he gave her a cuff on the back of her neck.

After he drove away, the heavy, early-morning was something she might have been nervous about, but she wasn't nervous. She had never seen so much fog in one place. The town below the hill was completely hidden, and so was the ground itself: it felt to Guida that she was walking in the air. Fog hung low in the old side gardens, and through the trees, and all around the house, like extra walls.

The sound of a handbell rang out just then from the house. It must have been the bell, Guida thought, for early prayers. The Grayfrocks must have been in the chapel. They must have been saying pre-breakfast prayers.

Guida entered the white palazzo. The urns in the vestibule were filled with flowers, tall and bright and colorful on spiky stems. An oak stairway, solid and curving and smooth, swung up from the lobby like the loop at the beginning of a spiral, with high banisters. There was a red carpet, deeply worn.

The rooms on the second floor were for retreatants, but there were no retreatants to be seen. Maybe it was a weekend of just the nuns. The nuns lived separately in another part of the house, which no one ever saw who didn't live there.

The white palazzo smelled like holy water, flowers, furniture polish, mildew, oatmeal, ashes, and old rugs.

Guida went slowly past the kitchen, saw no one, and continued walking slowly down the hall toward the lobby. She walked by the stairs into the silent, wide main room, holding the package of drapes in both hands.

Coochie had folded the drapes into a square block of fabric, and she'd wrapped it in waxy paper, like at the butcher's. The paper didn't crinkle because the outside layer of wrapping was a long white streamer of cloth, as smooth and as soft as perfect skin: someone in the army, a general, had commissioned Coochie to put satin linings in all his blankets, and Coochie had felt that he wouldn't make a fuss about it if a little bit of satin was missing. Guida had already imagined what it would be like to fall asleep at night with that material next to her skin.

The French doors at the terrace were covered with fog. It was a rich people's palazzo in every way. It was filled with beautiful wood. The chapel was off to the right behind a closed door with a plain wooden cross above it. The doors at the other end led into the dining room. Guida pictured smooth linen tablecloths, napkins the color of snow, and heavy silverware. She pictured herself living here, even though she wasn't a Catholic any longer. She would wear the gray dress and short veil, and though she had in common with the Grayfrocks that she wasn't good at sewing, she would sew her own hems, and theirs too, if they let her, she decided. She'd learn Spanish, and would love the palazzo as her home, as much as a proper Grayfrock. Whatever was asked of her, she'd do it, and she'd walk around the palazzo for the rest of her life as if she really belonged there.

She saw herself this way so deeply, she could almost feel the swing of a gray wool skirt at her shins. She went into the main room toward the entry of the dining room: then she realized that the nuns hadn't gone to the chapel at all. The dining room was full of nuns.

Four of the nuns, like an old-fashioned barbershop quartet, were standing by the long old windows, and the rest were sitting in chairs, like an audience, with their backs to the tables. The nuns by the windows were silent, but Guida had the feeling that they must have been singing. There was no sign of breakfast, and no sign that they'd already had it. The tables were bare and so were the sideboards. There weren't any instruments, but it seemed that music had been playing: the last of the notes were falling to the ground and disappearing.

An old nun, alone by the door like a bouncer, turned around and saw Guida, and her face flushed pink with surprise. She spoke English. "I never saw you before! Who sent you!"

Guida held up the white package of drapes. There were indentations in the fabric where she'd been squeezing it. "I have your silk curtains," she managed to say. "I'm delivering your curtains from Coochie."

The nun shook her head, and said again, "I never saw you before! Go and wait in the hall until we call you!"

When she turned away, instead of obeying her, Guida slunk over to the edge of the doorway and looked inside.

The nuns in the quartet took seats in the audience, and a short, plump nun stood up. Her face was light brown and deeply lined, like the shell of a walnut. She looked about sixty, but she might have been much older. She wore pointed, black-rimmed glasses. She looked so much like an owl, it seemed that a tan-skinned old owl flew in there one day, and had decided to stay, and had changed its birdy shape into this Grayfrock.

The nun wore her veil at the back of her head, and frizzy, gray-black hair spilled out around it. In her hands was one sheet of paper—not a piece torn out of a notebook, but something very formal, something official. She didn't look down at it. Whatever was written there, she knew it by heart.

The voice of the nun was quiet and somber, exactly the way it would sound, Guida felt, if an owl had started speaking.

"Now nothing else can be done. They have played their hand," she said. Then she said, "They are Irish."

Guida's heart thudded hard in her chest, then seemed to freeze. She thought that the owly Grayfrock was talking about the Irish nuns at school. Had Coochie called the Grayfrocks on the phone to tell them about the curse? Maybe she'd got it wrong, and all the Irish nuns would now receive it? Weren't nuns in retreat houses always saying prayers for outside people? Whenever someone in Guida's neighborhood died, their families wrote to convents or friaries with donations for special prayers. Maybe you could also make a contract for prayers-in-reverse. Maybe Coochie had contacted the Grayfrocks to deal with the curse in the same way Guida's uncle was a middleman in business, between the post exchange and his own customers.

But no, that wasn't what she'd meant at all. "They are coming here in five weeks. They want to turn it into a restaurant," said the Grayfrock. No one stirred; no one else said a word. Guida clutched the package of drapes a little more tightly, like a baby she could not let go of. Something very serious was in the air with the fog; she could feel it. If music had been playing, would it come back, would it sound like music being played at a funeral?

"A restaurant," the Grayfrock said again. The paper in her hand fluttered; her hand was shaking.

Just when it seemed to Guida that the word "restaurant" was the saddest sound she'd ever heard, and she would not be able to bear it if the sorrow in the room got any worse, another nun spoke up, from a row of chairs near the front. Guida knew from the sound of her

voice that she was very, very young. Her voice was light and buoy-
ant, and something about it made Guida think of colors like yellow
and white, instead of owly-gray, or black, or brown.

Guida couldn't see the younger nun; she wished she could.
Hearing her voice was like suddenly hearing a songbird with a
voice like the sound of a flute. What did she say? Guida didn't
know; the younger nun was speaking in Spanish. Up and down
went her voice, lightly, and it seemed to Guida that the lightness
itself was strong enough to drive out the weight of "restaurant,"
somehow, and, "they are coming here in five weeks."

It didn't occur to Guida to feel left out, or confused about missing all the meanings of the words. She didn't care what the younger
nun was saying. She listened to the sound of her voice as she would
listen to a bird, without stopping to wonder, "Now, in the language
of birds, what is that bird really saying?"

The owly Grayfrock stayed where she was and nodded as the
younger nun spoke. Now and then she frowned, or smiled, and at
last, when the younger nun seemed to come to the end of whatever
it was she was saying, the older one folded the piece of paper in
half, and put it away in her pocket.

The younger one must have asked her a question. "Yes," said the
owly Grayfrock, in English. "I know what their name is. It's
Gallagher, but that's not what they're going to call it. They are
going to call it White Cliffs."

The younger one repeated it. "White Cliffs." That was the last
thing Guida heard her say, but she didn't have the chance to hope
for more. As the younger nun said those two words, it was the
same as if she'd said, "abracadabra."

The fog that had hung so low all over the white palazzo scattered
backward. It happened so quickly, it looked strange and artificial, like
the blowing of fog from a machine in a Hollywood movie.

But it was real. The light at the back of the fog broke all the way through. Sunlight came through the windows in bits and pieces, in bars and half-circles, in shapes of eggs, in squares and diamonds, and in skittery, watery clusters. It was just like light through a prism, but instead of different colors, it was yellow and white, in different shades: yellow like egg yolk, hay, a flame, and butter, and white like cream, bread, ice, snow, and lightning.

Guida wasn't saying to herself, "Oh, the sun just came out." She was saying, "White Cliffs."

What cliffs? This was only a little hill. What kind of a name was that anyway? Was it Irish? How could it be Irish and bring this light? But that was what had happened.

Guida stood in the doorway transfixed. If a nun had caught sight of her and shouted at her to go away, she would not have been able to move, no more than a stick would. At the same time, she felt that something inside her was stirring. The package of drapes in her arms didn't muffle it. She had the feeling that something must have been sleeping inside her, as if, for who knew how long, it was asleep in a ball at the bottom of her rib cage.

At first she felt very disappointed. She had always thought that if she ever got to have an extra eye like Coochie's, it would be gentle and soft and well-behaved. It would have to be small and silent and round like a marble, like an eye was supposed to be.

She didn't know what to make of this, but whatever it was, it was wide awake. It was standing up inside her, straight up, and it was tipping back its head against the other side of her skin. There was only one thing it wanted to tell her. It was *hungry*.

Ten

"You ran out? You just took off? What happened to the drapes?"

"I left them on a table in the hall," said Guida. "I think someone saw me in the doorway and they came and closed the doors. I was scared. I didn't know what else to do so I put them on the table and went down to the gate and waited for my uncle. Then I went home."

"How fat were you exactly?"

"Pretty fat," said Guida.

She reached across the table and handed Tara a napkin. Tara had eaten three slices of pumpkin pie, hot, with ice cream, on top of a lunch of a fruit cup, a double cheeseburger, two orders of fries, and two chocolate milkshakes. She should have been drowsy and overly full, but she was wide awake. She felt she could still eat twice what she had.

She was bursting with more questions and they all began to swirl around in her head in a clamorous, unorganized rush. White Cliffs was a convent? The Gallaghers had bought the white palazzo from *nuns?*

And what about the school hall, when Guida was passed out cold from being hit in her seat, and she was out in the hall, too? What was it like to feel yourself in two places at once? When Guida unlearned the Catholic words, did the pictures she saw with her eye replace them? Did she still remember the face and eyes of the boy?

THE WHITE PALAZZO

What about that tailor? Did she know about the sunlight and the eye? Did she know that Guida had loved her, even though Guida hadn't said so? Did she die? Witches die, right? If so, of course she had to have died, for she was already old, she was ancient, when Guida was like, eight. When the old witch died, did Guida see it coming ahead of time, like a death foreknown, forewarned?

If so, did Guida tell her? "Coochie, at the backs of my eyes, I see that you will die tomorrow morning at ten o'clock?" What was *that* like?

And the drapes, did the Grayfrocks take them away? There had never been anything on the White Cliffs windows; there had only been glass.

And what about the younger nun? Should Tara be thinking of the younger nun? Why should she? All she had was a voice and it wasn't in English. Guida hadn't seen her face, yet she'd found her attractive. Should Tara tell Guida, "I picked up a lot of Spanish myself from my clients?" Why should she want to say that? Because it was something they had in common? Like, oh, we've both heard people speaking Spanish?

Tara was having a hard time with her effort to sort out her questions. She was trying to arrange them into four separate categories, like the four main points of a compass, but it wasn't working, because something else was taking place inside her.

Guida handed her a napkin. The last thing Tara had eaten was the pumpkin pie, and bits of the filling had stuck to a corner of her lips, like bits of orange lipstick. "Wipe your mouth," said Guida.

Taking the napkin from her hand, Tara found herself having to cope with a strong, internal force of shuddering. It was thrill and fear combined. She had the very odd sensation that, even as she tried to arrange her questions, something was rising up inside her to throw everything into swirls and confusion, with only one thing as a fixed, real point: Guida's hand, passing her a napkin. It was just a cheap paper napkin, the kind that's flimsy and coarse, both at once.

When Tara wiped her lips with the napkin, she wasn't sure she'd gotten them clean, so she dipped a corner of the napkin into her water glass. The ice cubes clinked lightly. The waitress hadn't been over for a long time to give them more water, but there were still some ice cubes in her glass, very small ones, all tinkly.

Something about the sound of the ice corresponded to something going on, all at once, in a very specific part of her body, at a definite point. It just now occurred to her that the point was like the point at the end of a long, thin banner or pennant. All of her body leading down to the point was only there, she felt, to be something that led to the point.

"Uh-oh," thought Tara. She had never felt this way before.

Oh no! What about her questions! What about the light in the White Cliffs windows, what about the floor that opened up to a tube in the center of the earth? What about the boy? What about the extra eye that came in through the window at the end of Guida's story?

It was the same as if the banner or pennant had all along, all its life, thought of itself as, say, a flag, in a smooth rectangular expanse, now and then ruffled, now and then shook, now and then folded up, and now and then wildly waving; and then suddenly it had to think of itself, unexpectedly, in a whole new way, as in, "I can't believe I'm a pennant. With a *point.*"

There was a part of Tara that coolly, calmly stepped back to take stock of this new situation, the same way she'd think to put her fingers on her heart if it abnormally started racing. At the same time, she asked herself, "How come I never felt this way before, and all she did was hand me a napkin?"

Once, Tara recruited a fifty-something-year-old man named Andy Simpson. Everyone called him Homer. He used to be an insurance adjustor so he needed to be placed in an office. He was ready for a temp job after three years of intensive AA, that is, AA every day of the week, and he was having some trouble with an unexpected side effect of sobriety. He wore the baggiest pants a man could get away with on an interview, but still, almost every time he walked into a room where another human being would meet him, he had erections, and they were getting in his way. It didn't matter that Homer had a new live-in girlfriend. He'd met her in AA and it was definitely a very physical relationship: they went to bed every night at about seven o'clock. But all the same, out in the world, as soon as someone started talking to Homer face to face, he would groan and turn around and walk out. It wasn't as if anyone could just ignore their own biology.

"Tara, you cannot imagine what this is like, not that I'm saying I'm not glad I'm a guy."

Homer took Tara into his confidence, on the telephone. He begged her to put him into the nuclear reactor plant, two towns over, just like the real Homer Simpson. Over there, everyone went around, even for interviews, in overalls and lead aprons, he imagined, and Tara had said to him, "Homer, you would set off the radiation alarms," and he said, "You're a girl. You don't know what this is like."

No way would Tara put a Fillins client in a nuclear plant, but one day, in the middle of winter, she happened to be recruiting in the employee cafeteria of a very large branch of one of the biggest insurance companies in the world (and not the one Homer had been fired from).

The heat in the building had gone off again, for the fourth or fifth day in a row, and it was freezing, and the generators were only strong enough for lights: the company was sick and tired of letting people go home just because it was zero, so everyone had to work in their coats. Their coats! Tara had raced to a pay phone and called upstairs to a supervisor who wanted some temps, and then she called Homer, and he drove right over and had his interview in his big wool winter overcoat and it worked out fine. All he had to do at his desk all day was never get up, even to go to the bathroom, without his coat.

Tara had never before in her life dipped a napkin in water to clean herself after a meal.

Meanwhile, Fuller's Diner was pausing in the act of being closed for the weekend. The kitchen people were through with the dishes; the floor had been mopped. Lunch was long over. Over at the counter, the weary waitress, in her jacket, with a purse on her arm, picked up a spoon and tapped it noisily against the cash register. "Excuse me," she called out. "If you're planning to order anything else, don't bother, and it's not because I'm throwing you out. It's because everything we had, you ate it."

"I want another glass of water with ice," said Tara, and the waitress said, "We're out of ice. We're out of water."

It was no use to try pretending that the point wasn't there. It was no use to try telling herself that she didn't understand why she compared herself to Homer Simpson.

The point was there, it was definitely there.

She felt worse than when her questions were careening out of control: she felt as if she were looking into a kaleidoscope that would not stop spinning, would not go away. She wished that Guida hadn't forgiven her about Major. She wished Guida had climbed over the cemetery wall as she'd meant to, and then a taxi would have appeared out of nowhere, like in a movie, like in a *horror* movie, and Guida would have climbed in the taxi and disappeared forever, which would have been perfect, Tara felt.

She thought she was going to start to cry, like a four-year-old, just burst out in tears. The effort not to made her feel that a water hose was inside her, like a hose filled with water, but someone had bent it, and nothing came out, not one drop.

"Your food is excellent," Guida said to the waitress. "The fish was perfect, and I would like to come back and try a turkey sandwich."

The waitress did not look complimented. The waitress looked as if, if Guida and Tara ever showed up again in the diner, she wouldn't wait on them.

Guida paid the bill—with money, no doubt, from that paycheck from Fillins. Tara's pockets were empty. She'd taken nothing with her when she had left the motel.

They went out to the parking lot. There was only one car; it was full of kitchen people. The waitress hurried out from a back door and squeezed inside, and they all drove away without a thought of Tara and Guida, stranded, with a closed-down diner at their backs, and not a phone booth in sight. It seemed to Tara that she'd left the Hathaway with Guida a long time ago. Why hadn't she bolted out the back door when Guida walked in? What was the matter with her?

She didn't cry, in spite of the pressure. She said, "You should have let me take my car. It's a long way back and my feet hurt, and we're marooned, like the people on *Gilligan's Island.*"

"Was that the one where they went off in a spaceship and got lost and could never go home?"

"No, that was just what it sounds like. That was *Lost in Space.*"

"I was never very good with television," said Guida.

Tara thought, "We have nothing in common, except that we both come from the same, stupid, boring, awful town." And she thought, "She is *old,*" and it seemed to her that there was never a time in her life when there was no such person as Guida Santucci.

Sometimes, she remembered, in the shadows of the plastics factory, Guida's small figure would come around the corner, a purse on her arm, her shoulders straight and firm in the clean crisp edges of a well-tailored jacket or coat; a silk scarf would be carefully arranged at her neck. She'd look something like an elegant European version of Mary Poppins. Behind the walls of one of the apartments in the blocks someone would be waiting to greet her, the Signora, come for a seeing to Johnson Street.

Tara would watch her approaching the blocks, crossing the scrubby little grass plots in front of the stoops, picking her way carefully in small steps. "You always look so nice, Signora," someone would always call out.

And Tara could remember herself watching the Signora with the hope rising up in her chest that hers would be the house she'd visit, with news of the future. "Come on in," her parents would have said. "Come and sit down and eat some sandwiches with us, cold cuts and cheese, and tell us what's coming."

There was no more kaleidoscope in her head, with churning, chaotic, bright blurs. It was the same as if it had adjusted itself to one picture.

Tara pictured herself as a child in the front doorway of her block, or at the edge of the parking lot, at dusk, with a red sun setting in the background, wondering why Guida went to other places, and not hers.

"Places," Tara thought. Places.

Some places she'd made love with Tommy were: his car, both inside and on the hood. And in his apartment building, in the laundry room, the back hall, and also in the elevator, stopped between floors, but only once, just to try it; and in every room of his apartment, including the water-heater closet and his bathtub.

Also, late a few nights at the top of the fire escape at Fillins (it just looked down on an alley). In her office under the table, on her rug. On top of his desk in the bank, not in the window, but after he was promoted to Mortgages. Eighteen or nineteen places along the river, both sides, and not just in summer like everyone else. Also, in every room of his parents' house when they took a vacation one year.

And at sunset on Saturday nights at the top of bare old West Hill, where an enormous, angling, orange sun would slide down the sky. All the houses below the hill would vanish in the glow, and she'd say to Tommy, "Look how all the houses disappeared."

Tommy would try to give her useful advice. "Honey, do you think for one minute, you could please stop looking at houses?"

But there weren't any houses in those sunsets, not even as house-like shapes. There were only people's windows. But for just a few moments, they weren't just windows at all. The sun suffused them and they were bronze, sun-oiled squares, all shiny and liq-uidy, like a solid and a liquid combined. As they filled Tara's eyes and made her happy, she lay back and wondered what it would be like if the person who was with her was seeing the same thing, was whispering in her ear, "Look at the sun on all the windows."

She had also made love with Tommy late at night in the break room at the plastics factory, where of course she knew the guards. And also in his car in two parking lots: the one at Wal-Mart, and in the back of the mall near the movie theater.

But not in the Mustang, not ever. Not ever in her car. And not at White Cliffs, not the hill, not the restaurant, not the fields, and not in the road at the bottom, as dark and deserted as it sometimes was.

Not at home, either, and it wasn't just because every night and every weekend, her parents were in the parlor watching television. She had never invited Tommy to her bedroom. Maybe he'd gone in there after she left home, but he never went into her bedroom when she was there.

She felt that, just because she didn't know at the time what she was saving those places for, it didn't have to mean she wasn't sav-ing those places, even though some of them were gone.

Her car, White Cliffs Hill, the fields, the road at the bottom of the hill, White Cliffs itself, and at home in the four rows on Johnson Street. And also her own bed. Those were the places she was *saving*.

It was beginning to come to Tara what she must have been saving those places for.

"I wish I had my car!" she said.

And in the road in front of the diner, what should appear but a ride.

"For crying out loud," said Guida. "Just what we needed."

It was the big old rumbly white Dodge van that belonged to Janey Hathaway of Hathaway the Florist, and it was slowing down with its engine all coughy and spurty, with a trail of gray smoke from a faulty exhaust. On the side it said in enormous pink letters, as pink as cotton candy, "HATHAWAY THE FLORIST, ARRANGE-MENTS, TRIBUTES, BOUQUETS."

"Hathaway," said Guida. "Like the motel?"

"This is a very, very small town," said Tara.

Janey Hathaway was alone in the van. She was older than Tara, well, in chronological years; Janey had already turned thirty.

There was a certain type of tomboyish girl, Tara felt, who wanted nothing in life except the chance to never grow all the way up, and this was what Janey was like. If a colt in a pasture could make a decision to never become a h - - - -, that would be Janey. Tara liked her. A lot.

Her hair was even shorter than Tara's. Her baseball cap was the same shade of pink as the sign on the van. She gunned the engine; the idle was like something about to die.

Janey tipped back the visor of her cap and yelled, "I've been looking for you everywhere! Get in! I got to make a delivery but first things first! Hurry up! You would not believe who's at my sister's!"

Guida whispered, "What sister?"

"This is Janey. Her sister Joy's my friend at the motel."

"I have a feeling," said Guida, "that Janey is going to tell you something you do not want to know, and neither do I."

Janey cried, "Your parents! Your boyfriend! Four people who, I don't know who they are! In the lobby!"

Tara looked at Guida for a long moment. "Did they *follow* you?"

"Follow me? But that's impossible. No, they could not have followed me."

"Joy said to tell you," cried Janey, "she did her best to tell them she never heard of you, but it didn't work! Do not go back to the motel!"

"Did they go into my room?"

"No! They wanted to! Joy and Dopey hid the keys so don't worry! Get in!"

They went over to the van. Guida whispered to Tara, "Is this safe?"

"Totally. You can ride in the back with the flowers."

Eleven

They rode along back country roads that seemed to go on and on without end, with twists and curves and turnings, all sunlit and coppery-orange. They rode west. The mountains of western Massachusetts were straight ahead in the distance, then left, then right. It seemed like a long time since the night Tara turned off the highway to find a town, when the sight of those hills in dusk and fog had made her panic.

Who could be afraid of those hills in daylight? Even at their peaks they were as rounded and smooth as someone's shoulder, and the lower, squatter hills were just like someone's knees. It was just as if someone had stretched out on their back one day by the smooth, upward tilt of the rim of the valley, and bent back their legs and made hills, and breasts too, and cupped hands, and elbows in sharp little angles.

The van was very noisy. There was so much clatter and constant jolting, they could have been riding in a cheap, rickety, nineteenth-century wagon from someone's farm.

Janey Hathaway felt like larking it up. A glowy sort of halo was around her, she felt: she liked it that she was playing the part of their rescuer. She turned her baseball cap backward, so that the visor was on the back of her neck, like a shield. She bore down on the steering wheel with a great show of competence and upper-body muscle, as if she were driving a semi, hauling lumber, instead of Tara and Guida and flowers.

Tara was in the passenger's seat. When her ears became accustomed to the noise of the van, she realized that Janey was singing, softly, so only Tara could hear her.

It was unbelievable that Janey was married to a man, but she was, and her husband—his name was Matt Hathaway—was the brother of her sister Joy's husband. Joy's husband's name was Mopey, like in the Seven Dwarves (he was really short, but the moping part was ironic; he was always cheerful). Janey and Matt had the floral business. Joy and Mopey had the motel.

The floral business was getting by, but not the motel. The motel was practically in receivership.

Janey was trying to get pregnant, Tara knew, but that didn't stop her from flirting with anything—anything at all—that stood upright on two legs; everyone knew this. Janey had played ice hockey in college, and she had also been captain of the cheerleading squad, for men's football. It didn't take much imagination to realize she must have looked great in a cheerleader's skirt, with those pom poms, and she must have looked equally great in a hockey uniform, even with a helmet on, and those guards you put onto your teeth.

Tara knew that there were many different types of people who had lost their heads over Janey Hathaway. Matt just accepted it; it was good for their flower sales.

What Janey was singing to Tara was the chorus of the golden oldies hit "My Little Runaway."

"Run-run-run-run-runaway," sang Janey.

"Cut that out."

Janey slowed down to let her shocks absorb a terrible shuddering and rattling from a bump in the road she had just gone over way too fast. Then she started humming the theme from the oldie television show *The Fugitive*.

"Cut it *out*."

"Sorry. I don't blame you if you're a little on edge."

And all along, the hills were in the windows on the side or straight ahead. There was not a way to not see them. All the knees and arms and breasts belonged to one body. The body that the hills resembled was Guida's.

"Your boyfriend is incredibly cute," Janey was saying. "I saw him through the window at the motel. He looked worried, but I think he was talking to Mopey about taking out a small-business loan. They must have liked each other right away because they're both so short. He has a really, really nice chest, very substantial."

"He is not," said Tara, "my boyfriend."

"Your fiancé."

"He is not my fiancé. You have to say 'was.' You have to put it in the past."

"I hope he knows what he's losing," said Janey.

"If he did, he wouldn't have lost me."

"Maybe. Maybe not."

"What's that supposed to mean?"

"It means, everything happens for a reason. I sell flowers to Buddhists out here all the time. There are all these Buddhists and that's what they say. Everything happens for a reason."

"Then why did White Cliffs burn down?"

"Because," said Janey, "maybe you needed to be lost."

"Well, I'm not lost now, not that I know where I am."

The flowers were piled high in bundles, in sheaths and loose layers of waxy, tissue-thin paper. There was a pile of pink and white gladioli, a pile of purple irises, a pile of pink and peach asters, and a pile of dark, ferny greenery, with leaf-spreads as wide as a kite. All the piles had needed to be piled higher, to make room for Guida, but she'd fit just fine.

As this was a delivery van, there weren't any seats back there, and there wasn't a carpet, just a white metal bottom with spots of rust. But there weren't any vases or containers to slide around or fall over and fracture her skull, say, or break her nose.

Guida had a very fine nose, Tara felt, and a very fine face: small, a little thin, a little angular, but not too much. Her complexion was not the white-bread-like paleness of people who do not get outdoors very often. She definitely looked, in fact, a whole lot younger than she was.

And Tara added something to the list she had started on the road from the cemetery. "Never get injured in any way." This went after, "Do not fall into crevasses."

The fragrance of the flowers was heavy and gorgeous, and they still gave off the smells of newly-cut things from a hothouse, with a dewy, sauna-like intensity.

Everything back there was soggy. If Guida complained about her clothes at the end of the ride—wherever it was that they were going—that would be all right too. She and Tara could go out to one of the malls for some shopping, although they would probably, Tara felt, never go into the same stores. They would have to split up and meet later.

Guida would want to complain about the roughness of the ride in the van. If she did, if she went on and on about aches, pains, rheumatism, gout, arthritis, or bursitis, which Tara knew everything about, from the partners at Fillins, well, she and Guida could find a Walgreen's and buy some aspirin. Or a package store and buy some wine—no, some brandy. The partners, being middleaged, preferred brandy for physical pains.

Did Guida like brandy more than wine, or both equally? What did she drink with her dinner alone in her house? Did she eat a lot of spaghetti?

Could she cook? Tara had never in her life cooked a meal, not even something where all you have to do is open a jar and heat it up.

Meanwhile, Guida was quiet. There was a window in the back, cracked open to let in air. It probably wouldn't happen that she'd suffocate. Did flowers give off oxygen, or suck it up?

"Janey," said Tara. "Do flowers suck up lots of extra oxygen?"

"No," said Janey. "Only I do." She was practically *winking* at Tara when she said this. What a flirt she was! But Tara wasn't about to protest. She liked it.

Guida's eyes were dark brown, almost black, like olives. There was an almond-like slant to them too, a very slight one. There were creases around her eyes, not many, and they were faint ones, not the type of wrinkles that dug into the skin of people over fifty who do not take care of their faces. Did she put lotion on before going to bed? Did she massage herself on the sides of her forehead, smoothing herself out, nightly, daily, three, four times a day? How many times a day did her phone ring? Was it always customers?

These were Tara's thoughts—not, "I put Guida in the back because it was not a possibility for her to be in the front with Janey Hathaway, who is immoral, unsubtle, and completely promiscuous."

But it wasn't that hard to imagine Janey glancing over sideways at Guida in a way she should definitely not do. It seemed as if a powerful, electrified current would shoot off Janey—or not just Janey, but anyone, anyone at all, who happened by—and poof, there would go Guida's heart, ensnared, captured, stolen, *gone.*

And she, Tara, would be walking around with nothing except the feeling that she'd been robbed of something she had wanted very much to not be robbed of—robbed badly, with that shock that comes on very hard, like a kick in the head.

She'd be saying, "I was robbed," all over again.

"Hey," said Janey. She tipped her head toward the back, to show that she was thinking about Guida. "She a new client?"

"Not exactly."

"She from your town?"

"I just met her."

"She related to you?"

"No. I really did just meet her."

"At the *diner?*"

"No, before. We were at the cemetery, and she didn't want to eat off the truck."

"Was it crowded?"

"Wicked," said Tara.

"She looking for a job?"

"She might be," said Tara.

"Well," said Janey, "whatever she's doing, and whoever she is, I think she's fast asleep."

There must have been a smooth patch of road underneath, or the van must have taken a break from all its creakings and groanings. It was just like the break between fits of someone with asthma, but in the pause, from behind the piles of flowers, they heard, very clearly—like the sound of the muffler, if the muffler had gotten inside—the sound of Guida snoring. She snored!

It was a relief when the normal van noises kicked back in. "Oh, great," thought Tara. "She snores."

"I can't believe I found you," Janey was saying. "I can't believe seven people are hanging around my sister's, waiting for you."

Tara said quickly, "Where's your delivery?"

"Stupid people from New York City," said Janey. "They've got a weekend place, they're wicked rich."

The snoring was blending into the rest of the noise in a comfortable way. Was there really enough air? Tara rolled down her window a little.

Janey whispered, "I think she doesn't have all her own teeth."

"Get out."

Janey gave Tara a shrug.

Tara said, "How can you tell if someone doesn't have their own teeth?"

"I deliver to nursing homes. It's something I notice. I'm vain about teeth." Janey lifted one hand from the steering wheel and tapped a finger to the clean, straight, perfect white teeth in her mouth. "All mine, in spite of playing hockey," she said.

Tara thought, "Even my parents have all their own teeth."

"What she's got, I would guess," said Janey, "is a partial. It's not the grossest thing there ever was. You can hook it onto teeth you still have, but in the nursing homes, they go for full-plates instead. The old folks jab themselves inside their cheeks or on their gums, with the hooks. Can you imagine how that must feel, on top of being old?"

"What kind of hooks?"

"Oh, you know. Fish hooks."

"I don't believe you," said Tara.

"You should. One time Joy had a fisherman at the motel who got a hook inside his cheek. He was pulling in some fish and the fish got off the hook and went back in the water, and he opened his mouth to scream at it and in went the hook. I was the one who drove him to the emergency ward. I could get him there faster than an ambulance. He still could talk, out one side of his mouth, and you know what he said? He said, 'I bet the fish that got away from me feels a whole lot worse than I do.' He had surgery and came out all bloated, with all these stitches, like his face was not the face of a human, but they didn't have to amputate anything. He was purple, but he still had all his face."

"Change the subject, Janey."

"I only mentioned her teeth because you're not supposed to sleep with them in. You would not believe what goes on in the homes when they forget to take them out. Partials are worst. You know how, with a baby, they put things in their mouth you think they'd never choke on, then they choke?"

Choking! What if she was not only almost suffocating? What if she was choking like a baby back there?

"Janey!" cried Tara. Her hand was already on the handle of the door. "Stop the car! We have to let her out! Stop this car!"

"It's not like she's locked in a trunk, Tara."

Janey was turning the van onto a dirt road that was lined with double rows of wide, beautiful hemlocks, all greenly furry and long-armed and solemn, with branches leaning down toward the ground, as if to touch it, and tops reaching up to the sky. The late-day sunlight and the dust made every hemlock look as sparkly as if someone had started decorating it for Christmas. Clouds of dust rose around them: Janey had slammed on the brakes.

But instead of letting Tara rush to the back to check on Guida, Janey took hold of her arm. Janey's face had turned a little pale. She said, "I forgot to tell you the rest of what's back at the motel with the seven people. I forgot because it's going to upset you. I just remembered because you said to stop the car, which I wouldn't have done. This is the road to where we're going. We're almost there."

In the back, the sound of the snoring had stopped, but one moment later came the normal sound of someone breathing, wide awake.

Tara said to Janey, "OK, tell me what else is at the motel."

"Your car," said Janey, miserably. "It's back from the shop. They came and delivered your car to the motel, and they gave the keys to your boyfriend."

Twelve

When Guida was in her prime, and doing seeings as often as she wanted, something happened to her that shook her so deeply, she came close to quitting seeings altogether.

The only reason she continued, besides the fact that there was nothing else for her to do, was that somewhere in the back of her mind she must have convinced herself that whatever happened to her for the rest of her life, in seeings or otherwise, nothing, but nothing, would ever be able to frighten her so badly.

Nothing "like that" could happen twice, she had felt. It was the same as if she'd accidentally shattered a favorite glass bowl, or went out and put an ax to her crabapple tree, then said afterward, "A bowl in pieces on the floor can't ever be broken again," or, "Now I'll never have to look at that tree." If she'd loved the bowl or the tree, it wouldn't have mattered. They'd be equally gone, regardless of her feelings.

So when something "like that" happened to her for the second time, in the back of Janey Hathaway's van, on a country road some-where in the west of Massachusetts, with the humps and peaks of the Berkshire Mountains in the window—the one little window—well, not only was it as bad as the first time, it was worse.

She would try to make light of it later. She would talk about the awful van, the way the fern stems poked into her stockings, the way gladioli were on her head, and irises were all over her, like a blanket.

She'd say, "I thought I was dead when I woke up in Janey Hathaway's van because of all the flowers."

The first time it happened was in the men's prison, but at least she'd been sitting upright in a chair, a straight-back wood chair, with her eyeglasses on and her feet planted squarely in front of her. The chair had been loaned to her from a friendly guard. It had no arms to hold onto, but she was anyway, out of habit, gripping the sides.

She always gripped the sides of chairs that weren't armchairs when putting on a seeing. It was an old, old habit, because she knew what it was like to be a child knocked out of a chair by a grown-up: knocked way, way out, to fall down a hollow through the center of the earth, which perhaps would have no bottom.

When she put on seeings, it was something like passing through the hollow to a place, like an actual place, that she thought of as "the other side of the hollow," but she didn't need to fall sideways out of a chair to get there. When the guard brought in that chair, she asked for something with arms and he said, "Signora, you are a very classy lady, but this is a prison, not the tea room at the Ritz."

She was allowed into jail cells like chaplains and lawyers. One day she did a seeing in the cell of a man named Morris Kerrigan, who'd gotten into a bar fight one night and killed a man named Barry Haines with his fists. He was up for parole. It wasn't murder, it was manslaughter.

For some reason she did not have her usual detachment. Instead of paying attention to Morris Kerrigan, who in fact was a mild, gentle man, with a cell full of books, and walls full of colorful prints mailed to him from art museums, not the usual pornographic pin-ups—well, she must have been distracted. She must have been wondering about the bar fight. She must have been paying attention to

Morris's fists. She must have been tired to begin with, and she knew a few people as customers who were relatives of the slain man, Barry.

When she was getting near the end of the seeing, she realized she didn't know where she was, or how she had gotten there, or what she was supposed to be doing. One minute she was saying, "Morris, what I see is, if I put in a good word for parole, you need to move somewhere else, where Barry hasn't got any family."

Barry Haines had been a linesman for the telephone company and his four sons, who had loved their father, were perhaps not completely to be trusted. Two of the sons were karate experts. "Do not go back to town," were the words on Guida's lips, when suddenly, a sense came over her that she had been hit, very hard, even though there was no pain.

She felt as if she'd been hit between her shoulders, but instead of tumbling down into a hollow, she was stuck at its bottom (there was a bottom). Everything that was real—the man who was seated in front of her on the side of his bunk, in his prison clothes; the pictures on the walls; the sides of the chair she was gripping; the thoughts she had been forming and the words she had been speaking—seemed insubstantial, somehow, and far, far away.

There was no sound, in spite of the fact that in the middle of the day, a prison is never quiet. It was as if her powers to hear, and to see, and to feel, were gone. It was as if all of the workings of her body, including the pumping and circulation of her blood, the ticking of her pulse, the feeling of being weary, the pang of hunger she'd felt just a moment before in her belly, had come to a stop, as truly and fully as the engine of a car can suddenly seize up and be frozen. And she was sorely afraid.

She had the horrible feeling that her eye was the only thing still working, as the battery of a car can keep operating when the engine is dead. She was the same as a dead-engine car that still had its

THE WHITE PALAZZO

headlights on, still had its radio playing, still had the sound of its horn. She felt that her eye was continuing without her. It just kept looking and looking, indifferently, like a surveillance camera in a store.

It must have been a long time she sat there like that. What was her eye looking at? It was looking at the bottom of the hollow.

What did the hollow look like? It looked empty. How could something be empty, and still be seen? She didn't know. She only knew what she saw. There was no other way to explain it.

She didn't know where she was, she didn't how she'd gotten there. All she knew was that she was looking at something that was empty, from inside it.

She'd been aware of feeling chilled, as if she'd been sweating, and someone had just turned on an air conditioner, which was blasting at her. The prisoner, Morris, must have called for a guard. A guard had come running. What was told to the guard? She didn't know, but it was probably, "The fortune-teller seems to be having a problem getting up from her chair."

Somehow she'd made it out of the cell, out of the prison, out into daylight and sunlight and things to look at that were moving about normally: things that were real.

"Where *am* I?"

The shapes outside the window were shapes of mountains. What mountains? These were not the hills of home. Someone was talking. Who?

Something was brushing against her forehead, against her lips. She wondered if she were out in her yard by the pear tree and mosquitoes were flying around her. She couldn't tell if she was breathing, or not. If her nose were still in place on her face, she didn't know it.

The little window filled up with white, white sky. She had never been in an airplane. She wondered if perhaps she was in one now.

She wondered where it was going. She wondered if she'd buckled herself into a seatbelt. She couldn't seem to find a way to move any part of her body to check.

And she felt that if her heart were made of stone, it would have sat in her chest with the terrible stillness of her own human heart.

The sight of the sky had gone out of the window. There wasn't daylight, but there wasn't darkness, either. There was nothing outside the window at all. It was glass. It was clear, unclouded glass. She was looking at glass, and in the glass, she saw the glass. There were no reflections, no flickers of light, not even one tiny bit of a shadow. When it came to seeing through it, there wasn't any "through."

It was the same as if she were looking at air itself, and even as a part of her brain was saying, "It is not a possibility to look at clear glass without seeing something through it," she knew that, that's exactly what she was doing, and all that remained to be resolved was why.

She knew she wasn't blind. Her senses were gone but she could see. There was only one reason for the things that were happening to her. She felt no regret or sadness; she felt no satisfaction or relief. She felt no particular hopefulness, but she wondered if she'd ever look at anything again that wasn't empty.

"I am dead," she concluded.

As if to confirm this, there appeared a set of shapes outside the window. These shapes appeared to be walking toward her. They were shadowy, loose, and large, as if approaching her slowly, in a floating, windblown way, as if they were walking very high above the ground, as if their feet were on a floor made of sky, cloudless and sharp and clear and clean. Late-day sunlight was behind and all around them, in orangey-yellow shades of autumn, like the color of pumpkins.

Guida could see that she was right about the shapes outside the window, but they were not ghosts. They were trees. They were long-armed, greenly drooping hemlocks, standing thickly together. It was very, very quiet.

"Where *am* I?" said Guida. And to her great surprise, this time she had an answer.

A voice said, close by, very clearly, "My *car.*"

The stone in Guida's chest that had taken the place of her heart was the same as if someone had kicked it. It gave a funny little jump, and turned back a moment later into a pounding, simple heart.

Guida knew that voice. "Well, Janey, as soon as we deliver these flowers," Tara said, "we have got to go rescue my car."

They had come to a stop at last, a proper stop, with the engine off.

They had bumped and swayed along a narrow dirt road, deeply rutted, and now that it was quiet, Guida couldn't tell if those background sounds of sighing were coming from herself, or from different parts of the van.

"Let's get this over with." Tara said this—to Janey, Guida thought—as she was opening the back door. Guida thought she was talking about unloading the flowers, but here was Tara, and she was kissing her.

Marvelous van! What a marvelous van this was!

First, the back door opened wide, and dusty, sunlit air came rushing at Guida, with a thick smell of hemlocks. Then Tara was rushing in too, grabbing at flowers and pushing them aside, as if she were digging her way to Guida in a very big hurry.

It was a good thing Guida was already lying back and wedged in place. Tara flung herself at her so hard, she would have tipped Guida over sideways.

It could have seemed that all she meant to do was express to Guida a quick, girlish, spontaneous rise of—of what? Of some emotion. She might have been sitting in the front of the van with some emotion building up inside her, and simply chose Guida as the receiver of its manifestation, as a dog, in a happy mood, will jump up and lick the face of whoever happens by. It wouldn't matter to the dog at all if the face it licked was the face of a perfect stranger.

It was not a wet kiss. It was dry, gentle. It was not accidental, it was deliberate, which was obvious because, as soon as it ended—as soon as Tara drew back and took a breath, as a swimmer does—she bent right back down toward Guida and parted her lips, just slightly, and pressed her mouth on Guida's again, a little longer this time, with a great deal of feeling indeed.

Under Tara's knees, stems and leaves were being crushed, and that was how it felt to Guida's lips, that they were crushed, just perfectly crushed. She could feel the tip of Tara's tongue, but she felt too stunned and too shy to do anything with her own mouth except to keep it tightly closed.

"There," said Tara. "That is totally out of the way."

Then she said, "If that wasn't OK, well, it's OK with me, I mean, if it wasn't OK with you, I won't ever do it again, OK?"

"It was all right," answered Guida.

Once, she did a seeing for a man named James Sabatini. He was sixty and he was about to have heart surgery. She did the seeing at his bedside, making room for herself among the tubes and bags he was attached to.

He had wanted to know if he was going to die on the operating table and, if so, would he go to heaven or hell?

This was not a question Guida was afraid of. People asked her this all the time. She knew everything about James Sabatini because he grew up in the Italian part of town. He was a bully, a thief, a deceitful husband, a show-off, a liar, and a vain, hard-hearted miser, who had never in his life done a thing based on warmth or affection.

Flat on his back with his head on a hospital pillow, he was a scared, small, pale, frail man, whose family wanted to be rid of him so much, they were all out shopping for black outfits to wear to his funeral, but still, as much as she felt sorry for him, Guida also felt she'd have to be honest.

"You are going to die, and you are going to go to hell," she had said. "But you've still got about ten minutes before they come to take you to the surgery, so, what do you want to do about it?"

"Hold my hand," he answered, and she did.

She felt that, when people say the old saying of how your life flashes by in the instant when you think you are dying, they should add, "It also passes by the eye of your fortune-teller, if you are lucky enough to have hired one."

At the end of James Sabatini's ten minutes, when a nurse was coming in to fetch him, he blinked his eyes open and looked at Guida and said, "I am totally different! I feel like Scrooge! Signora! Scrooge! The three ghosts did it all in one night! You're just like those three ghosts! But with me, it only took ten minutes! Signora! No shit! I feel great!"

In fact he did die, in the recovery room, right after his surgery.

Why was she thinking about him now? Was she worried about hell, like a natural, leftover side effect from being Catholic? Was that it, hell? Hell because Tara had kissed her, hell because every single fiber of Guida's being—her hair, her skin, her bones, her muscles, her legs in the stockings that were torn, her pounding heart, the tips of her fingers, the bottoms of her feet, everything—seemed to only exist for a moment in the future when kisses would come again, and more than kisses, too?

Maybe there was no such place as hell. But if there was, and if hell was a place she would go to for kissing Tara Barlow and wanting more, she was willing to go there.

"We're ready for you," said the nurse to James Sabatini.

What had happened when Guida let go of his hand? He said to her, "Signora, lean down," and she did so, bending her head to the pillow like a priest, as if she'd come to hear his confession.

Then James Sabatini turned his face to Guida, and lifted his head slightly, and kissed her on the mouth, warmly and softly, like a lover. Guida remembered how the nurse tapped her foot on the floor and looked at her watch, waiting for the kiss to be over.

This had happened eight or nine years ago. It was the last time Guida had been kissed. It was the same as if her lips had a memory of their own. But until Tara kissed her, she'd never, ever felt like Scrooge on that Christmas morning, when everything was completely transformed.

And Tara was a *girl.*

They were out of the van. Janey was coming toward them. The house they had come to, at the end of the dirt road, at the end of the columns of hemlocks—at the end of the world, it seemed—was an old gray stone cottage, so small that there couldn't have been more than one room inside. The high roof peaked steeply; it was checkerboarded with light and dark slate squares. Ivy covered the walls, thick and healthy and shiny. There was no garage, no car, no telephone, no electric pole. There weren't meters for gas or water. The shutters on the small windows were closed, but smoke was coming slowly, languidly out of the chimney. The small lawn in front was well-cared for. There was a flagstone path leading to the front door. It was as free of weeds as a carpet.

"This place looks like Grandmother's house, like in 'Little Red Riding Hood,'" said Janey. "I hope Grandma has some cash, because someone's got to pay me, and I never take credit cards."

"Neither do I," said Guida.

"And what is it," said Janey, "that you do?"

"I'm a . . ."

THE WHITE PALAZZO

Tara did not poke Guida with her elbow, but she looked at her as if she had. "She's unemployed. She doesn't take credit cards because she has no job."

"We could use another person in the greenhouses," said Janey.

"She is not," said Tara, "botanical."

Janey switched her baseball cap so it wasn't backward, as if that's what she always did to make herself presentable. She went into the van on her hands and knees and began to sort out flowers.

"Here, you might as well help." Janey handed Guida a sodden bunch of irises.

"They got a little crushed," said Guida.

"You probably didn't do it on purpose," answered Janey. "If I thought you did, I'd send you a bill, but don't worry. The crushed ones can go on the bottom."

Guida held the flowers close to her chest. What she wanted to do was let them drop to the ground. What she wanted to do was reach up to Tara and put her hand at the back of Tara's neck, in the spot where the blonde-white hair tapered off into a small, fuzzy "v," like a miniature version of a man's goatee.

Then she'd lay her hand at the back of Tara's head and bend it toward herself, exactly as if reaching for a pear in her pear tree, as if pulling the pear to her mouth while it was still on the branch. What was the good of two kisses—two only!

Once she did a seeing for a woman named Helen Macomber, who had a daughter named—she couldn't remember the daughter's name. The daughter was twenty and she was taking cocaine, a great deal of it.

The girl had gone into a coma.

She was put in the county hospital. Guida went and sat with her and afterward, when the girl woke up again, Helen Macomber wanted to know from Guida if the coma was an act of carelessness.

Was it an accidental overdose, or was it deliberate?

She had wanted to know if her daughter had been trying to die. Guida told her exactly what she saw. She saw that the girl wasn't interested in suicide; it was the furthest thing from her mind. She very much wanted to keep living because of all the cocaine she had not yet had. When she thought about "being dead," all she thought about was the cocaine she'd miss out on.

Guida remembered what Helen Macomber's face was like when she said to her, "Your daughter has something to live for, but it's cocaine."

"I'm addicted," thought Guida. "It only happened five minutes ago, and I'm addicted like Helen Macomber's daughter."

She was still alive. Kimberly, that was her name. Guida remembered seeing her one more time, and it was in the county hospital, again. Not long ago she had walked by a door, on her way to another client, and Kimberly's name was on the door.

It was the coma unit. Guida had not gone inside—she hadn't been hired to—but now she wished she'd stopped in. She wished she'd sat with Kimberly. She knew perfectly well that there wasn't any comparison between a killer drug, and the act of kissing Tara. But all the same, it was definitely something to want to stay alive for. She wished she'd been able to communicate to Kimberly that someday, she might understand herself how she felt.

Thirteen

A light wind was blowing. In the shadows of the huge, rustling hemlocks, where the branches were swooping and waving, like long, dark-green streamers, it seemed as if the scene in front of them—the little cottage, the road, the trees—was the background for a show on a stage, and the curtain had just gone up.

"I feel like I'm watching a show," Tara whispered to Guida.

"I've been feeling like that myself."

The front door of the cottage opened and a man and a woman came out to the stoop, in evening clothes—in *evening* clothes, as if they were leaving for a night at the opera.

And at the same time, from around the back, there appeared a very odd little man, whose clothes were so strange, and whose size was so small, he could have been one of those ceramic little gnomes, which tacky, really suburban people put on their lawns and in their gardens.

He came toward them at a run, stopped abruptly, and threw up his arms in the air. He cried out, "Signora! Signora! How I wondered if my eyes were telling lies!"

Beside Tara, Guida froze.

"Darling," said the woman on the stoop, to the man. "I thought you said you ordered them in vases."

"Darling, I thought you said you wanted them spread out on the floor," said the man.

"But that was for later. We haven't got any vases," said the woman. "We can bring the flowers inside, but we have got to have vases to put them into, so we can take them out."

"Darling, I thought you wanted to keep the cabin rustic."

"Fuck, fuck, fuck, they want vases," said Janey.

"It's our anniversary, and we are going to have a party," said the woman, to Janey. "We came from Manhattan, and we haven't got a car, because we sent our driver away. This is our summer house."

"Signora! Signora!" cried the little man.

He was coming toward Guida, and Guida turned away from Tara, and seemed to forget all about her.

Tara's sense of being a spectator intensified. She had never felt comfortable at being part of an audience; it made her too nervous to not understand what she was supposed to be watching.

The woman and the man on the stoop—rich people from New York City—were throwing themselves a party, and it was obviously a party for just two. They were standing there all dressed up, and everyone was talking at once, and Janey was upset, and these different things were so vivid and disconnected, Tara felt as if she were back in her life as a child, sitting on a bench between her mother and father, at a circus.

She'd been brought by her parents to a circus, just that one time. Not knowing where to look, and feeling dazed and confused, she had lowered her head for all of it, in spite of how expensive the tickets had been, and in spite of the way her parents, one on either side of her, had poked her and prodded her and begged her to watch. How could someone not look at a circus? And the ride out of town to the circus grounds had been a long one, and she'd never been brought anywhere before, and they'd gotten all dressed up.

She remembered what it had felt like to not know where she was supposed to be putting her eyes. She'd looked down, staring hard at the north of her toes in her shiny, Sunday shoes, and then at the south of her heels, and then to the east of one side of one foot, and to the west of the other.

No one had told her a circus had three rings. She'd felt proud and happy that she had survived it. No one knew what was happening with her, but when she finally raised her head, the circus was over, and there was nothing to look at but sawdust, animal droppings, and big, brightly-colored blocks that could have been for jugglers, or acrobats, or elephants, or clowns.

North, south, east, west. She had missed the whole circus, but she had figured out how to make herself a compass.

That had been the first time: she remembered everything about the way it had felt to place herself in the center of four directions. The difference between having and not having a compass was like the difference between breathing as if she'd just been running hard for five miles, and breathing as if she and the world around her were together in a single, calm unit of stillness.

Now she felt as if she were the one who'd been running from the side of the cottage, not the strange little man who was taking Guida away.

His face was as brown as a walnut. His trousers were wool, a tweedy wool, and they were held on his skinny body by a pair of leather suspenders, thick and wide, like a harness. The bottoms of the pants were tucked into his boots, so they looked jaunty and loose, like the jodhpurs of a jockey. The boots were the boots of a workman, with steel-plated toes. The plaid of his flannel shirt was not quite the same as his cap, but it was close.

Obviously he worked there. He worked for the man and woman on the stoop. But he only had eyes for Guida.

"Mr. Dunfee," said Guida, and the little man *beamed*.

"Signora, you're a long way from home."

"Mr. Dunfee," said Guida, "so are you."

"But I thought, when I saw it was you, you might have forgotten me, for which I wouldn't blame you at all. So many years have gone by."

The change that came over Guida was so remarkable that, if Guida's very skin had changed color, or if her hair were rearranged, and along with her hair, the alignment of her nose and eyes and mouth, Tara would not have been more surprised. Her voice was different too: a liquidy, ripply sort of undercurrent had entered into it, so that it almost seemed like she was singing.

"I could never forget you, my dear Mr. Dunfee. If the day should ever come when you suspect that I did, may that day be the day I've lost my memory completely, and not only my memory, but also my mind itself."

"Ah, Signora. May that day never arrive."

"Peppy!" called the woman on the stoop.

Peppy, what kind of a name was that? Look at the way his eyes were on Guida! He was slouched a little, so that his face was level with the button on her blouse that was exactly in the middle of her breasts.

Tara had the strange sensation that the smallest person there was herself. She felt she must have shrunk, like Alice in Wonderland. She wasn't used to feeling shorter than other people, especially when one of them was almost a dwarf.

And what was Guida saying to him—no, singing to him? She was telling him, "Of course I'll go with you, seeing as how I'm here, Mr. Dunfee. I am sure I can spare you an hour."

The woman and man on the doorstep were about the same age as Tara's parents. She thought, "Except for being rich, they could be my parents. My *parents.*"

A hard little nugget of guilt and remorse was forming at the back of her mind. It wasn't bothering her too much, but she knew

THE WHITE PALAZZO

that sooner or later, it would, the way a blister takes shape on a toe or a heel, and before it gets painful or starts to pop, you can still keep walking on it.

She thought of the dozens, no, the hundreds, no, the thousands of times she had begged them to let her get them jobs somewhere else, anywhere else but the factory. All they'd ever said to her was "no." They were too dug in where they were; they were waiting for their pensions; they were looking forward to what it would be like to retire and get paychecks for staying home.

Tara thought of what her mother looked like when she came home from her shift. She thought of the way her mother stripped off her clothes when she was barely into their apartment and rushed into the shower: her scented soaps and fruity shampoo never quite got rid of the smell of burning plastic.

She thought of the way her father always had to stoop and duck his head to go through doorways. She thought of the way he sat at the table and peeled an orange with a knife so that the peel came off in one piece. The skin of his hands was grooved and rough and gritty. He was supposed to wear a protective eye shield at the machines but he was always taking it off, as if that were the one thing that made him feel he was in charge of his own fate.

His eyes were bloodshot from the plastic dust. The part of his eyes that manufactured tears no longer worked. Once in school, there'd been a story about a man called the Sandman who entered people's houses at night and sprinkled sand in their eyes to make them slide off to sleep and have happy, colorful dreams. A teacher had read it out loud. Only one child in the room went pale and trembled with fear, and it was Tara. "It's magic sand!" the teacher had assured her. "No one's scared of the Sandman." But Tara knew what it was like to look at her father's dry, pink-shot eyes.

Her mother had told her that working at the machines without an eye shield was like being in a desert with your eyelids glued open, in a windstorm, every day.

Tara thought of the way the partners were always saying to her, "You have nice, very sociable parents. You are a giant question mark when it comes to the laws of genetics."

Whenever the partners called her at home, her mother and father used their nicknames, which was something they'd never do to their own bosses except behind their backs. The phone would ring and they'd say, "Hi, Bone," or, "Hi, Ax." When the partners came over at Christmas to give them a wreath—the partners gave everyone wreaths at Christmas because Robocop had a brother who had a tree farm—her father would go to the door to let them in and call out, "It's Ax-and-Wee-and-Bone-and-the-Terminator!" He said it the same way Tara did, like it was all one name. He never called Robocop Robocop. He called him The Terminator because he thought it was a much better film.

The wreath for her parents wasn't just a wreath made of free pine cuttings. There'd be all these little green and white and red and silver bows. Tied to the pine with the bows would be ten-dollar bills, maybe ten, maybe twenty, and they didn't make a big deal of it; they just acted like the money was bits of tinsel. Did they give her a Christmas bonus? They did not, and they didn't even let her have her own wreath. They'd say, "You have a bigger bank account than we do, so buy your own."

Her parents! "I probably seem like a terrible, selfish, self-centered, hard-hearted daughter, and I'm the only one they've got, and I love them, and I have got to stop avoiding them, because it's totally, totally cowardly," she said to herself. At the same time, she was thinking, "Maybe I can be cowardly a little longer."

"Tara!" Janey nudged her. "What's the matter with you!"

"I don't know," said Tara, which was the truth. She felt that she

THE WHITE PALAZZO

was traveling in strange new mental directions, and her brain kept spinning out of control, being flooded with memories, sensations, new thoughts, all at once.

"These people are way rich," said Janey. "Don't you think they look like Barbie and Ken, middleaged? While you were just standing there in a daze, not helping me with the flowers, they paid me. They gave me a ten-dollar tip. In cash, but now I have to go back for the vases. I thought they'd be nasty, cheapo, Scroogey rich people, completely plastic."

"Maybe they are," whispered Tara.

All the flowers had been put inside. The man and the woman were holding hands.

"You're so sweet to go back to town and I'm sure you'll hurry back," said the woman to Janey.

Pearls were around her neck. Her dress, no, her gown, was like the blue of the darkening, late-day sky. It was strapless and full in the skirt, and her arms were long and bare. If a Barbie doll were five-feet six inches tall, and about fifty years old, with silvery-blonde hair done up in stupid little ringlets around a face that was plain, very plain—even homely—then there she was.

The man beside her was wearing a black tuxedo that was just like a tuxedo worn by Ken. His hair was slicked back; it could have been hair on a doll. He resembled the woman in his plainness. He had just shaved. Tara could smell his cologne across the yard.

Who cared if the man and the woman were like dolls? Who cared who they were? Tara felt herself pulled toward the door of the cottage, which made her nervous, as if her curiosity to go in would get the better of her. She felt homesick; she felt alone. She did not feel that it was right that Guida had turned away from her, as if erasing her.

She had to stand very still and wrap her arms in a crisscross at her chest, pressing her hands against her shoulders, as someone would do who had just been discovered to be naked. She felt like walking into the cottage like Goldilocks and trying out the chairs. What was this like? It was almost like wanting to go inside White Cliffs.

It was already too late to say to herself—as she'd been doing every day, sometimes every hour, for the last five weeks—"Don't think about White Cliffs."

But this time it didn't come into her head with smoke and ashes and grayness and darkness, like a picture that was taken with x-rays.

She could remember exactly what it was like to never worry where she ought to be putting her eyes whenever she found herself in the road at the bottom of White Cliffs Hill—at six, at seven, at fourteen, at twenty, it didn't matter, it was always the same. There was only one place to look, and that was up. She'd look up, and the hill would be filled with White Cliffs, with nothing else there except the sky and the light and maybe some snow, and the wide, yellow, beautiful hayfields. Had her mother and father taken her for drives on that road? She couldn't remember.

But they must have. How else would she have seen it so young? Who else would have brought her there? There'd been no one else.

"We'll drive by White Cliffs, and we'll never bring you to a circus again," her parents must have promised. They must have noticed that she had wasted the price of her ticket on looking at her feet.

When did her N make the leap from the points of her toes to the mansion on the top of the hill? She didn't know. There was no first time White Cliffs was N.

"Come on, Tara," Janey was saying. "You have to come with me to get their vases."

But Tara wasn't going anywhere without Guida.

"If you don't come with me, and if you're not right here in this yard when I come back with the vases, you are totally on your own,

Tara, because I'm not going out looking for you again later on, in the dark, as I happen to have a husband I would like to go home to, if that's something you would care about," said Janey.

Tara turned her back on the van. Too many things were churning around inside her; too many waves of feeling were competing for her attention at once. "What I need," she told herself, "is a compass."

The sun was behind her. West. West was where the sun was. East was the door of the cottage. South was the van that Janey was driving away in. South was back at the Hathaway. South was where everyone was *waiting* for her.

North was Guida. North was where Guida was walking away: she was following the little man toward the woods at the side of the cottage.

How could she have thought she had a choice about a direction? How could she have worried where she ought to be putting her eyes?

"I feel," Tara said to herself—and she was breathing a whole lot easier now—"like Luanne Wheeler's pigeons."

Luanne Wheeler was a lab technician further up the valley and her hospital had closed. Tara had found her a long-term temp job at the community college, where someone was doing experiments on pigeons. Luanne had gone out there for the interview and came rushing back to Tara's office one hour later, almost screaming.

Instead of taking the job, she had wanted to free the pigeons. She wanted Tara to come and help her. The experiment, Luanne said, was about placing the pigeons in a long, narrow box, the bottom of which was divided into lanes. Electric grids were set into the base, and the pigeons had to walk through the box to reach food in little dishes at the other end.

What kind of dishes? Little silver troughs, but that wasn't the point. If the pigeon rushed madly out of its lane, in an individualistic way, a shock would be applied to its feet.

Soon, except for a couple of deviants, they'd march to their food in straight lines like soldiers after two weeks of boot camp.

That was how the man who was running the experiment had put it. Boot camp. When the experimenter turned off the electrical currents, on they still marched. The average number of times you would need to apply electricity to the twiggy feet of most of those birds, before they'd walk in straight lines forever, was five or six. This was what the experimenter called "learning."

No, they couldn't break in and free the birds; the college would sue the partners. The pigeons probably would not have been able to fly. They had probably had their wings clipped.

Tara had called the Red Cross and got Luanne a job instead with the Blood Bank. But she had thought of those pigeons a great deal.

What about the deviants? Luanne had never mentioned the pigeons who, shocked a few times with an electric jolt, just stood there and refused to move at all: they'd prefer to go hungry. But there also must have been pigeons who'd learned how to dodge a few jolts, and they would rush even faster down their lanes, as if the jolts they received would be worth it once they got to the dishes. Maybe it was boring, bird-food pellets. Maybe it was something fantastic. Luanne never said what kind of food was in those dishes.

"Guida! Wait for me!" cried Tara.

She followed Guida who followed the odd little man. Guida looked over her shoulder just once, and said nothing to Tara, and didn't seem to care if she was there, or not.

They didn't go far from the cottage—just into a small clearing in the woods. Tara knew enough to keep quiet. She had a good idea what Guida had meant when she'd told the man she'd give him an hour.

His name was Harold Dunfee.

Maybe the seeing that Guida put on for him didn't count as an actual seeing. Guida sat down on a rock in a mossy, damp patch of woods behind the old stone cottage: she took her eyeglasses out of her purse, put them on, and sat there and nodded her head now and then. It didn't seem like she actually paid attention to the things Mr. Dunfee told her.

Also, technically, it couldn't be thought of as a proper seeing because Guida wasn't accepting any money for it. Did fortune-tellers have standards and codes of honor, and channels for making customer complaints? No, they did not. It was a completely unregulated profession.

But it wasn't as if Tara could stand back and judge her, in the clear, cold light of reality, as someone who was doing something that was immoral, deceitful, and an outright act of trickery. If Guida had tried to talk him out of wanting a seeing—if she'd tried to excuse herself by saying, "I have lost, Mr. Dunfee, my third eye, and I'm afraid it's not a temporary condition"—he would not have believed her. Or if he did, he would have sat down anyway on the ground at her feet—at her feet!

"Lie to me, Signora," he would have said. "I would rather have you lie to me than not speak to me."

They didn't call him Peppy at the cottage because he was spry and energetic. Sometimes he had terrible dreams of being set upon by big, brainless thugs, who would stroll through these very woods one day while he was pulling up weeds or hosing off bird droppings from the flagstones and, without a word, they'd put a bag on his head and sedate him, and he'd wake up in a bed in a nursing home and the thugs wouldn't tell him where his pants were, or his shoes.

The pep was a front. He was seventy-six years old but he was passing himself off as less than sixty. But when it came to his true age, he explained, he really felt it.

Tara found herself wishing she had a mirror. She wished she had taken the time to look at her own reflection in the mirror of Janey's van. She felt sure that something in her face must be different. She felt sure that the face of Tara Barlow that had never kissed Guida before would be gone, and in its place would be the face of a brand-new Tara Barlow. She'd felt sure she'd notice the difference right away, even if it was a cheap, no-good mirror.

It would not have been possible, she felt, that a difference would not be there. It wasn't as if she expected, say, a little sticker or tag on a corner of her mouth, like a sticker at the grocery store on an apple or a banana, saying, "These are happy, happy lips." Was kissing a woman different from kissing a man?

Yes. It was totally, totally different.

"Susie Rawlins!" Tara thought. "Oh no!"

A couple of months ago, she'd put a nineteen-year-old girl named Susie Rawlins in the Holiday Inn as a functions waitress and one day the general manager called up Fillins to complain: he had asked for some *babes* to wait tables for his conventions, so what were they doing sending him a guy?

Tara had gone over there. She barged in to square it off with the manager—that was part of her job; she was always going out to stick up for the partners, like their bulldog—and, to her amazement, Susie Rawlins was standing there in a snazzy pair of satiny black pants and a white shirt: under the shirt her chest was as flat as a board.

Two days before, in Tara's office, Susie Rawlins had presented herself in a flowered dress, with an elastic, prim headband holding back her very long, very wild, curly dark hair. The dress was short; her legs were perfectly shaven, or waxed.

But her hair had been cut so that she looked like a long-haired boy. She was muscular enough to pull it off. She even had an earring in one ear, and she smelled like men's cologne, and on her feet were shiny black dress-up men's shoes. "Hi, Tara," she had said. "I'm ready to start saying I'm a guy now."

"Your outfit is fantastic," was the only thing to say, and that's what Tara had said.

She had thought at first that Susie Rawlins was trying to make a point, in a political way, about the fact that it is illegal to consider a person's sex when deciding whether or not to hire them, and it would have given her a great deal of pleasure to mention this to the general manager, but no, Susie was turning into a boy. Where were her boobs? In the flowered dress her breasts had been high and firm and large.

"Those were my falsies," she confided, right in front of the manager. "I already had my real ones removed."

"It must have hurt," said Tara.

"Not as bad as it hurt to have them."

That was as far as she'd got in talking with Susie Rawlins. The manager took her away to fill out tax forms, because of course she—he—was keeping that job. The next time Tara went out there, the manager told her Susie Rawlins had been recruited by another hotel chain, which regularly sent spies to steal his people.

She really had looked like a boy. If Tara hadn't seen her as a girl, she never would have guessed that she had been one. And her voice had changed too. She had sounded like a boy whose voice was delayed in changing. How could that be?

Why was she thinking about Susie Rawlins? "Falsies." Was she thinking about falsies because of Guida's teeth? How many teeth were the false ones, and what about those hooks?

But why was she picturing that flat, boy's chest? What about Susie Rawlins's breasts? Were the real ones small and undeveloped, like a boy's, to begin with?

The fact remained that in Tara's eyes, Susie Rawlins's breasts had looked much, much better when they were on her, even if they'd been artificial. Her poor chest! Would hair grow there? And what about the rest of her? What was between her legs?

Tara sighed. Then she thought, "I am not turning into Susie Rawlins. I am not, not, not losing *anything.*"

Meanwhile, Mr. Dunfee kept talking and talking. "If I was still a Catholic, and if my knees weren't so bad, I'd be here on my knees saying thank you to God out loud, Signora, for putting you not only on this planet in general, but all of a sudden, right out of the blue, after all this time, God is crossing my path with your own."

It occurred to Tara that there must have been a reason for the sudden appearance of this old friend of Guida's—well, maybe not friend, maybe a former customer—and the reason would have to do with herself. It seemed to her that this was just like a sign, but not a sign with any particular message. It was the same as if Mr. Dunfee had appeared to really hit her over the head with the basic, irrefutable facts of people's ages.

He was incredibly old—so old that, beside him, Guida looked as if she were blooming with youth. And where did that leave Tara? It left her with the feeling that numbers were being flashed before her eyes, on a sign.

"Twenty-four!"

And then, "Fifty-three!"

And then, "Old old old old!"

Tara thought, "This is so abnormal. When Guida's as old as the funny little man, I won't even be as old as she is right now, but many, many years will have passed."

She thought, "Guida is fifty-three years old."

She thought, "Do the math." What was fifty-three take away twenty-four? Twenty-nine, but instead of saying to herself, "She is older than me by almost thirty years," Tara said instead, "Twenty-nine take away twenty-four is five," which made her feel a lot better, as if in actual fact, at the time when Tara was born, Guida hadn't started the first grade.

Did you still get periods at fifty-three? Did Guida still get periods?

Tara couldn't just ask her. She couldn't interject herself into the business at hand between Guida and the little man, saying, "Do you menstruate?" Or, "When you're at home alone, do you take out your teeth, or keep them in?" Or, "What is your house like? What is your bedroom like? What kind of a bedspread do you have? What do you wear to bed? A nightgown? What kind of a nightgown?"

She thought, "I should try to put my mind on higher things."

Peppy, they called him at the cottage. He was old. They called him Peppy because they made it up that he was Mexican. They thought all groundskeepers in America were Mexican. The man who had worked at the cottage before him was an Armenian, and they had called him Juan, so it wasn't just with him. They weren't racist, he explained, just stupid.

He had no complaints about the people he worked for. He had no complaints about leaving their town, his street, his everything: he liked it out here near the hills just fine, and anyway, no one from his old life was left.

For himself, back in the old days, far away from here on the other side of Massachusetts, had he ever been a complainer? Had he ever once complained about the rotten bad-luck things that went on in his life, his whole life?

He wasn't complaining about loneliness, either. He had a nice apartment in the next town. He wasn't lonely. All he was, he felt, was *done*.

And he wasn't complaining about his ailments although in fact his digestive system was failing; he ate oatmeal like a baby and for animal protein, all he could handle was broth from out of a can.

The light of day gave him terrible headaches; his lungs were weak; there was cancer in his colon. If the bladder in his gut were a part of the plumbing in a kitchen, the pipes would be leaking, the faucet would be corroded, and the drip, drip, drip would drive anyone crazy, and when it came to his mind, it was just like the sun in the sky slipping down off the edge of the world at twilight, except that the sun would come up the next day, and his mind, once set, he had realized, would not.

He only had one thing to complain about: his heart, which kept on going. He felt that if his heart were a clock on the wall, and someone smashed it with a sledgehammer, it would still keep ticking out the minutes, without sense, without meaning, without hands, without numbers. There'd be nothing left of him but the little bit of hearing he still had left in one ear, and there would be nothing for the ear to listen to except this hollowed-out, disembodied ticking.

Ticking, ticking, ticking, and the light of his mind going out, and thugs from a staff of a nursing home in his dreams. That was how he put it.

Ha! Tara was sitting on the ground at an angle to Guida's rock. She looked over her shoulder at the smoke in the air from the cottage chimney. Did the man and the woman at the cottage have a pension plan for him?

Probably not. How could she have admired their house and failed to see that they were slime? If you overlooked the nut-brown, sun-colored skin of his face, Mr. Dunfee was as Irish as a picture of a leprechaun. That would be the reason behind "Mexican."

"Our illegal Mexican alien" must have been the phrase in their minds, which was the same as saying, "Our consciences are clear about being totally Republican with our alien about employment compensation." It was nice for Janey that they were lavish with florists, but slime was slime.

In the meantime, explained Mr. Dunfee, there was still just time enough for him to see things clearly. Please, would it be, after all, such a terrible thing if, one day, perhaps soon, he went out by himself to one of the hills to stop living? In a woodsy spot, he'd dig himself a hole, and make sure he never got out of it alive.

"Living," said Mr. Dunfee, "I don't mind telling you, has had its ups and downs for me."

Did Guida recall how he felt about outdoors? If she remembered him at all from the old days, that would be the thing she'd remember of him the most. He had always felt his best outdoors, and he wasn't only saying this because of the four years of doing time.

Jail! Was that why he'd let the man and the woman get away with the Juan and the Peppy? It was better to play the part of an illegal than the part of a guy with a record?

Jail for what? Tara knew from her own clients to never ask this question out loud.

"I was a reprobate," Mr. Dunfee said. "I never gave a thought to the consequences of a single one of my actions, beyond the large satisfaction it gave me to be committing those actions, which, if I had to do it all over again, I wouldn't change a thing, not counting the four years when they had caught me and hauled me off. All the same, I never did a thing I'd go to hell for, and I would like to keep it that way, if you don't mind."

He'd been busy forming his plans for his future. He'd be careful to pick a spot where there weren't any hiking trails. He might, as his last act of physical activity, not counting the activity of passing out of this world, dig himself a hole to get into. He wasn't interested in delaying much longer.

Soon it would be late in the autumn. He knew what would happen if he put it off until winter. He'd sit there ready to die, but the minute a little chill came into his bones, he'd lose the nerve and get up and go home. He didn't like the cold. Even with a bottle of bourbon he would not be able to stick it out; he felt certain of that.

He was willing to run the risk of wild animals. People said that there were cougars in the hills but no one had ever seen one; same with coyotes and black bears.

And there were foxes, skunks, porcupines, and wild turkeys. But if anything came sniffing at him, it would be deer. It would not be that bad of a way to go out, he felt, with noses of deer up close to his clothes, and nothing in his eyes but the sky—the unrestricted, unbounded, wide-open beautiful sky. He wouldn't care if big-jawed, sharp-toothed animals appeared at the top of his hole and crept in and attempted to maul him. He wasn't afraid; he'd bring a knife. All he cared about was that he went out of this world in the quiet and peace of a hole, looking up at the sky. "When you're done, Signora, you're done," said Mr. Dunfee.

Tara pictured him with a shovel. When Guida was as old as Mr. Dunfee, would she want a hole, too? Would she take out her teeth—probably, they'd all be falsies by then—and put a shawl on her shoulders, like a witch in a book, and walk out the door one day, and call over her shoulder, "I'm going downtown to the hardware store to buy a shovel"?

Maybe she wouldn't put on a shawl. Maybe she'd put on a sweater. What door would she walk out of? Oh no! Who would be there to hear her? Who would be there to rush after her and grab her by the arm and make her keep staying alive?

THE WHITE PALAZZO

Fourteen

Guida did a seeing once for a retired army nurse by the name of Myrtle Hasselbad. Myrtle spent the years 1967 and 1968 in Vietnam.

The seeing took place in the front room of Myrtle's little wood cottage by the river. Myrtle had insisted on having twenty or thirty candles—the scented kind, vanilla and strawberry and almond—which was oppressive. But the windows were open. The smell of the river was sharp and close. Myrtle was having flashback visions of war. OK, she'd taken LSD, a lot of it, she'd been young, who hadn't?

But this wasn't about LSD. She'd gone on leave from her job at the county rehab. Sometimes she heard the roar of helicopters when nothing was in the sky. Sometimes the river looked molten and burning, like a river of lava.

"Signora, please, stop this war." She wanted Guida to get rid of her memories, in one hour.

Myrtle put Guida in a low chintz armchair by the window. The river wasn't on fire. Guida watched the candlelight on her tired, pinched face. There was always a moment when, on the edge of going out of herself and going into another person—that was the only way she knew to describe it, going into another person—she'd wonder, "Would this be a time to hold back?"

All the old fears of what could happen to her would rush back to her. This happened often when she was starting a seeing.

Maybe this was the way fishermen felt when they'd been at it for a very long time. They went out to the shore and looked at their ocean, in the gray-white light, before dawn. "Should I go out there today? What about these waves? What about this wind?"

It was never a question of wondering if the time would come when she left herself and didn't come back, which was irrational. Fishermen who looked at an ocean on a regular basis as something that would probably drown them would not, she imagined, last very long at their jobs. You either went out there and fished and took your chances, or you didn't. You had to forget about the dangers.

She was every bit as practical as fishermen. The only thing that was important was the moment when the decision was made to either shove off into the waves and take her chances on what she'd find, or stay on land. After the decision, nothing could be done to undo it. But she had never held back before.

Myrtle Hasselbad was a whole new experience. This wasn't the first time Guida had been called for a seeing about a war that, in the history books, was over, while in life, it was still going on. She'd done maybe twenty, twenty-five seeings involving those vets. She'd seen a lot of what they had seen. She had never flinched or held back before.

Maybe this was because Myrtle was a woman. Before Myrtle, she'd only had combat vets. She had looked those other times through the eyes of soldiers, all men, not through the eyes of a woman. She'd been able to have some detachment.

Or maybe it was the candles, flickering and smelling like candy. Or maybe it was the way Myrtle sat in front of Guida. Myrtle had pulled up another chair and put it down so closely to Guida, their knees were almost touching, as if Guida had brought a Ouija board, and it was sitting between them on their knees. Guida liked it better when her customers were on the other side of the room.

— 164   THE WHITE PALAZZO

Or maybe it was because Myrtle had gotten so fat.

It was summer. Myrtle had on a thin cotton dress; the dress was paisley and sleeveless. She'd gotten so fat that every time she spoke, or sighed, or seemed to feel something deeply, the floppy extra flesh of her upper arms and the fleshy loops of fat around her chin and her neck and her hands started rippling and jiggling and swaying.

She was barelegged. Unlike the rest of her, her legs were not fat. There was mostly the whitish, pale, unnatural flatness of skin grafts, as if someone had taken strips of latex gloves, or bits of a deflated white balloon, and glued them onto Myrtle.

"Napalm did this to me," Myrtle explained. "I took hallucinogenics because, to put it bluntly, what I saw when I was tripping on LSD made a whole lot more sense to me than what I saw of what went on in Vietnam." How could Guida do a seeing on this person? But she couldn't just get up and walk out, not with all those candles, not with the way Myrtle tipped back her head and smiled at Guida bravely, as if Guida were a dentist. Guida had wanted to touch Myrtle's legs. She had wanted to feel that skin. She didn't want to know how the napalm had got there, or what the air was like, or how water of a river could catch fire. Guida just wanted to reach down and run her hands up and down Myrtle's legs, as if she wore pantyhose that were a little too loose, and needed Guida to smooth out the wrinkles.

It had actually crossed Guida's mind to say to Myrtle, "Stroking legs is part of how I do seeings." This had embarrassed her.

But she didn't want to know anything personal about Myrtle Hasselbad. She didn't want to see what Myrtle had seen. She didn't want to know what Myrtle knew.

It was the same as if Myrtle had brought her to the entrance of her triage tent, and Guida had followed her in. But unknown to Myrtle, Guida was blindfolded, say. And her ears were stopped up with ear plugs, and an oxygen mask was on her face, as if she refused to breathe the outside air. Of the many things Myrtle described to Guida, Guida remembered nothing, because she hadn't heard a word Myrtle said, and she hadn't caught one small glimpse of the things that Myrtle had shown her. It had frightened her because it was so easy. It was her one act of cowardice, and her one act of cowardly, hard-hearted fraudulence, both at once.

All along, while Myrtle thought a seeing was going on, Guida looked out the window. It was the only way she could keep her eyes off Myrtle's legs. She couldn't see the water from where she was, just the willows on the bank.

She knew them well. They were the same trees she'd sat under, long ago, on Sunday afternoons in the summer. The sloped, grassy area where the willows were wasn't part of the sandy public beach. Everyone called it "the Italian section," as if the neighborhoods of town would have to be replicated at the shore.

The river had been clean enough then to swim in. She had never learned to swim, but now and then, Guida would get up off her blanket under the willows and make the effort to go down to the water. She never wore a bathing suit. Fat girls never did. So she never had to worry what people at the beach might think of all the layers of extra, heavy flesh she really had. She had kept herself covered, no matter how hot it was.

But she never left the shelter of the willows. She would sit there instead until everyone else went home. There were a couple of places in those beautiful old trees where the branches grew so thickly, no one could see inside. No one could see her when she was there, not anyone on the beach or in the houses nearby, or in the water, paddling by on a raft or in a rowboat. The branches of the willows were like long, streaming curtains. They were just like curtains made of leafy, green hair.

That was what Guida looked at, and thought about, and remembered while she sat knee-to-knee with Myrtle Hasselbad. She thought about what it would feel like to touch her legs, and then she thought about herself as a girl who hid in trees, and how she never had worked up the nerve to go down and put her feet in the river like everyone else.

At the end of the seeing, Myrtle said, "Thank you, Signora," and rushed to get her purse to give Guida a tip. Myrtle didn't know yet that after Guida left, the helicopters would keep hovering and roaring, in a sky where other people just saw clouds. And every time fog was on the water, she'd say to herself, "That's smoke from aerial bombing."

She had never called Guida again. Guida knew from the other nurses that she had never gone back to work. What had happened to her? Back in town, the cottage was empty, and it was falling apart. Surely the dereliction had already started happening before the seeing. It had been shabby, a little moldy, a little creaky, but Guida had not looked around very carefully.

In fact, Myrtle's cottage had turned into an eyesore. The roof had collapsed, the windows were broken, and the sturdiest pineboards of the outer walls had been removed, perhaps by someone who was building a cottage of their own. Or they'd gone out in the back of a truck, to be sold in a scrap-wood junkyard, who knew where. Through a gap in the north-facing wall, you could see where someone had ripped out Myrtle's kitchen sink. Someone from the Department of Public Works had told Guida that they were planning to go over there and clear out the remains with bulldozers.

The tip from Myrtle had been sixty dollars. "An extra dollar for every minute," Myrtle had said. "I'm sure you're worth it."

It was the biggest tip Guida had ever been offered. She took it. And when she spent the money later, she didn't feel guilty about it.

She had wondered if something might be wrong with her conscience. But at the same time, she understood that faking Myrtle's seeing was something that, sooner or later, she would have to account for. She felt lucky that it was just the one time.

What about the seeing she'd done, or hadn't done, really, about Tara? She had gone down to Johnson Street. She had looked at photos. She had listened to people describe her. She had looked at Tara's narrow, small bedroom, at the cartons stuffed with plans for her wedding, at her clothes, at her sheets, her pillow, her bed. She had taken money from the Barlows. But it didn't count. It didn't count because you can't do a proper seeing on someone who's not there, which she had carefully explained to Tara's parents (but they had wanted her to try anyway). And it didn't count because, what had she said to Tara's parents?

"I'll try again, alone, at home," she had said. "You've given me a great deal to go on."

And she had said, "I will find her."

She had made up her mind that she would never stop looking for Tara until she found her, for real. It was certainly not a conscious decision. She never even gave it a thought, although now and then she told herself, "Since the fire, it's not like I have anything else to do," or, "I have to honor my promise to the Barlows, Don and Dell, the two bells."

She never said, "I want to hold the girl in those photos I saw in my arms."

She never imagined holding Tara in her arms until after she had walked in the door of the Hathaway. And even then it was vague and shapeless, like imagining holding a blanket.

She didn't doubt her conscience about the way she'd set out to find Tara. She'd been professional about it, through and through. She had made some lucky guesses, such as, "she would never leave

THE WHITE PALAZZO

Massachusetts," and, "she'd go west," and, "I think this girl is more interested in White Cliffs than in a wedding, never mind being actually married."

They'd been *guesses*. Her conscience was clear. Right up to the moment when she walked into the Hathaway—one more motel to go and check on, and one more looming, potential disappointment—all she was doing was her job, even though she was doing it in a way she'd never done it before. That was how she had explained it to herself.

The seeing on Myrtle was different completely. It was just like a debt on a credit card. It would never go away until she paid it. Guida had known all along that the moment would arrive when suddenly, she'd find herself thinking of Myrtle very clearly—her legs, her scars, her dress, her skin, her helicopters. And Guida knew that, when it happened, she would feel that she was back in Myrtle's chintz chair, with scented candles burning all around her, and nearly suffocating her.

She also understood the basic fact that when that moment arrived, it would come at her out of the blue, probably at a very bad time. And she knew that when it presented itself, she would recognize it right away.

And here it was.

It was almost as if she could hear Myrtle's rough, sad voice, as if Myrtle had come to the door of the cottage to let her in, as if Guida had just arrived, as if the seeing with Myrtle hadn't happened.

"How's it going, Signora. Come on in. This place is no palace but I've got two good chairs, and I bought a whole bunch of candles." That was what Myrtle had said.

"Signora! Signora!"

The small, dark-skinned, stubby-faced old man who appeared out of nowhere, and came rushing toward Guida on stiff, old-man legs, was some kind of workman, Guida saw. She thought he was shouting because part of his job was to scare off trespassers.

But no, he knew her. He wasn't shouting at her because she hadn't read the posted trespassing signs. He wasn't saying, "See, see, see," as in, see the signs? He was calling her "Signora."

"Signora! Signora! How I wondered if my eyes were telling lies!"

Over their heads, twilight was settling into the trees like a dark, greenish-gray blanket. The window shutters of the cottage had been opened, and the lights from inside threw out square, shimmery reflections among the shadows.

Harold Dunfee. That was his name, Harold Dunfee.

This was payback time for Myrtle? Now? It had to be, or she wouldn't have felt that she was seeing poor Myrtle so strongly. Guida didn't even know where she was.

And it wasn't as if she felt she had a choice. All she could do was be still like a fisherman in gray, cold air at the edge of the sea. Would it happen, would she feel it all over again—that catch in her throat, that catch in her heart, that giddiness, that fear, that joy, that *pull?*

"Uh-oh," she thought. "It looks like I'm going fishing."

But Harold Dunfee? Why should Harold Dunfee have turned up? He was miles from home, but then, so was she.

There had to be a reason. Had he been in the military, had he gone to Vietnam? No, he was too old. Was he wearing something paisley? No, he wore plaid, he wore flannel, he wore wool.

Back in town, had he lived by the river? No, he hadn't. Had he been fat, like Myrtle? No, he had always been as slim as a jockey. Were their families related? No, they weren't. Did their families ever know each other? No. Harold had a sister and a brother and a couple of aunts, but they had all moved out of the valley when Harold had started out in his career.

The Hasselbads, years ago, had a sausage factory, which went bankrupt after the end of the second world war. They'd had a big white colonial two towns over, near their factory; the cottage at the river was their camp. The only Hasselbad left had been Myrtle.

Guida couldn't remember if she'd ever had Harold Dunfee as a customer. There had been so many. Sometimes their faces blurred, all swirling and confused, exactly as if her memory were the tube of a kaleidoscope, and someone was turning it.

Harold didn't have a chair for her like in a proper seeing. He offered her a rock. She had never done a seeing outdoors before, not that she was calling this, officially, a seeing.

"Payback," she called it.

"Wait for me!"

Tara, flushed and indignant, was rushing after her, kicking up pebbles and dirt. Guida touched her fingers to her lips and thought, "Tara."

And she remembered something about Harold Dunfee in a flash.

Prison, she remembered. He'd been in the cell next door to Morris, the man who had killed another man, whose seeing was such a nightmare to her. He'd been on his way back to his cell. He wasn't in for murder or manslaughter, just car theft; he had the run of the place.

She remembered all over again what it was like to be alone at the bottom of the hollow, with nothing working except the unwavering, glinty stare of her eye. Harold Dunfee had looked into Morris's cell, and noticed that the Signora was in distress, and had called a guard to come and help her.

Guida almost laughed out loud. Maybe Harold Dunfee had been sitting in his cell with the hope she'd go next door and do a seeing on him.

Well, it looked like his time had come at last, sort of. How could she call this a seeing when she didn't have her eye, when it was gone for all time, like White Cliffs?

Fifteen

Guida realized that she did not feel deceitful about putting on a seeing with Harold Dunfee. But if Harold Dunfee, or Tara, gave Guida a quiz to see if she'd paid attention to actual words he had said, she would flunk it. He talked and talked and she did not listen to a word of it.

She understood him, though. She got the gist of it. He was old, he was lonely, and he felt that his heart was his enemy because it wouldn't stop beating. The only thing that made him happy was the thought of himself in a hole, with his eyes looking up at the sky.

Tara. Guida only looked once at Tara as she sat there. It took a great deal of effort to not pay attention to the last of the day's yellow sunlight in her hair, and to not think about what happened in the back of the van. And to not keep looking at the curves of her chin, her breasts, her elbows.

Guida knew what would happen if she wasn't careful, if she wasn't professional. It would be Myrtle Hasselbad's legs all over again.

She just wanted to make sure that Tara was there. She wanted to make sure that she had not imagined Tara Barlow. What color was her hair in the thin, fading light? It was the color of hay that's been partially covered with snow. It was tawny, like cat fur. It was corn-like, like silk and husks, and like corn on the cob that's called "butter and sugar." It was lemony. It was white and blonde. It was silver. It was yellow. It was downy.

She was sitting there. For real. Guida held one finger to her lips in the gesture that means, "Be quiet," but all she wanted to do was touch her own lips lightly, as if something of the kisses still lingered.

Then she looked very carefully at Harold Dunfee. She watched his face. She watched the air turning darker among the shadows of the giant trees.

What a very strange world this was, Guida thought. What a strange, strange world. She remembered what it had always been like to have her eye, and think that nothing was ever strange at all. She remembered what it was like to never be surprised at anything that happened that seemed astonishing. People told her astonishing things all the time.

She looked at Tara out of the sides of her eyes. She remembered what it felt like to have her eye. She remembered what it felt like to feel *lucky*.

She bowed her head. She wondered what it would be like to be much, much farther from home. She wondered what the sky would be like—the wide open beautiful sky—if she decided one day to set off by herself, walking north, straight up along the axis of the world, walking and never needing to stop until she made it as far as you could go.

Once she did a seeing on a man who grew up in Alaska. He had fished for salmon for a living and his eyes had seen the great northern lights. Guida remembered everything of the way the man had described them—in words, just words.

She had gotten inside that man, all right, but when it came to seeing the colors, something had failed her; she only saw the usual sky. The man had told her that the northern lights were the closest thing on this earth to things that are not of this earth, and it didn't matter at all that they were really just outpours of gas, simple gas, and some odd-colored vapors from the sun.

She remembered the name of the salmon fisherman's old boat because it was the same name as the saint she had picked for her confirmation. She couldn't remember what confirmation was about. It was a sacrament, and everyone had to choose a patron saint; that was all she remembered. She already wasn't a Catholic, but as she had to go through with all the motions—and they didn't let you graduate to high school until you did—she was careful about making the right decision on a saint. It was a sort of attachment that only went on, in a one-sided way, in one's mind.

The salmon fisherman had wanted Guida to try to do a seeing about what had happened to his boat, which he loved. The only reason he had sold it was that another boat, with a crew of six, had come apart in a storm and had sunk, with no survivors.

One of those six had been his wife. One of them had been his sister. The other four were his four best friends. As soon as the sixth funeral was over, he packed up and sold everything he had. He had driven his boat to a marina—he couldn't remember which one—where a dealer gave him eleven hundred dollars in cash. The boat was worth thirty. What had happened to his boat?

"I don't know," Guida had answered him. "But I can see that, whoever has it now, they didn't change the name. It's a good one."

Teresa was the name of the boat and the name of the saint.

The Teresa wasn't Therese of Lisieux, in France. It was Teresa of Avila, in Spain, the home of the Grayfrocks.

Therese of Lisieux, the Little Flower, Guida had felt, was simple-minded, as if a mind were like a bud, and as easy as a bud to understand. People who liked the French Therese probably had a fantasy that the world always lived in one season, which was spring.

THE WHITE PALAZZO

You were never supposed to pray to Teresa of Avila, who was said to be strange, intellectual, a hysteric, and probably insane, even though she was the founder of the famous order of nuns called the Carmelites.

If there ever had been a Catholic saint who acted the opposite of what Catholic saints were supposed to be like, especially as models for girls, it was the Teresa who wasn't French. She had gone around telling Catholics that, if they wanted to talk to God, they should talk in their own voices, their own words, in any way they wanted to do it. She did whatever she pleased. She had the bravest heart of any saint Guida had ever heard of.

She reminded Guida of those women who lived in caves in Rome, long before Jesus. They were the ones who had given oracles.

In the pictures in schoolbooks, they had long gray hair, as stiff and dirty as bristles on a broom. They had never in their life used a comb. They wore rags and hid from daylight like lepers, but when they opened their mouths and tipped back their heads and delivered bulletins, from the minds of pagan gods, they really sounded like gods.

When it was time for Guida to write the name of her saint on the official Confirmation form, she boldly wrote "Teresa."

No one had ever mentioned it. Maybe she'd gotten away with it so easily because the nun who taught religion that year thought that Guida had meant to pick the Little Flower, but her spelling was wrong, as if naturally, children of Italians could never be cured of using vowels, and would always—obstinately—put an "oh" or "ee" or "ah" or "eh" at the ends of all their words.

She wished she'd been able to tell the man from Alaska where his boat was. She wished she hadn't had to say to him, "You need a computer, not me. You need to be making lots of phone calls, not sit here talking to me." She'd refunded his money.

"Thank you for telling me about the aurora," she had said.

It was twilight. She felt that the edges of the ordinary world were slipping away from her, the way objects on shore slip away when you are leaving a harbor in a boat.

She'd always felt that evening was the best time of day for a seeing, and it wasn't only because she liked to be offered dinner at her customers' tables. Evening was when everything paused.

Twilight in the evening, she felt, was different from twilight at dawn. They were two different colors of grayness. It didn't matter what season it was. It didn't matter where, either. It was a difference of coming and going, and of those different shades of gray—not around the edges, but straight up, inside the bowl of the sky, before sunrise or sunset seeped all the way in.

She liked to wake up early. She liked to measure her days by first one dusk and then another.

Morning twilight was paler, and always took her by surprise. The grayness of outgoing darkness was thinner, like smoke from candles. Evening twilight was like something that's descending. The gray was the gray of a sidewalk of newly poured cement, or a slab of natural slate. The first light of morning, she felt, was like something being lifted. The grayness of morning twilight was like a cover, or a lid, or a blanket, which someone was lifting, say, and pulling off you, and even the stupidest canary in a cage in someone's kitchen would know the difference between its last sight of light after supper, when its cage was being covered, and that first crack of light the next morning, when the cover was taken off.

The sun was down behind the long, high hills to the west. It was far too early to see stars. Smells of cooking were in the air—nearby, someone was cooking. There was a smell of toasted wheat, and with it, a smell of chimney smoke, a little acrid, a little bitter.

Soon enough, it would be winter. Guida thought about the way that soon, in the evening twilight back in town—back home—houses would be lit up with Christmas decorations.

As early as the first or second of November, people's windows would fill up with the lights of electric candles, lighted wreaths, miniature plastic sleighs with red bulbs around the reindeer. And there'd be lights from a Christmas tree in a living room, and blue and white flickers of television sets, with that strange, unreal glowing.

And the streetlights would all look different, too, and so would people's porch lights, and their car lights, too.

"Lights," thought Guida.

She wondered what everything back in town had looked like in the days when the streetlights were gas, and when there weren't any streetlights at all, and when lights in the houses only came from wax candles.

She never decorated her house for Christmas; she never had the time. Christmas had always been busy for her. Once, two of her neighbors—a married couple, young and new to the neighborhood—came over with a bunch of red velveteen ribbons from the Hallmark store at the mall. Each of the ribbons had been tied into a small circle, like tiny bow ties, or lassos, each with a miniature bow.

"These are for your crows," said Guida's neighbors.

No, they weren't bringing over the ribbons because they were trying to say to her, "The crows in your yard are driving us crazy. We want you to strangle your crows with these nooses." They had felt she would enjoy the idea of having them decorated.

They had wanted her to know that they thought of her as someone who would love to look out the window and see crows fixed up for Christmas in red bow ties.

What were the names of those neighbors? They'd moved away. She remembered that she had given the ribbons later to one of the nursing homes, where they were given as one-day-only bracelets to thin-wristed old women.

She didn't remember the neighbors' names, but she remembered what it had felt like, when they came to her door with their gift, to have wanted—just for an instant—to invite them to come inside. She almost had done it, in just a simple little phrase, "Please! Come inside! I'll make tea!"

But it wasn't a strong enough impulse. The moment passed. She never, ever invited her customers or her neighbors—who were often one and the same—into her house.

She didn't feel she had anything to hide, and she didn't feel, like a turtle, that her house was like a shell, and hers alone. It was simply a rule, professionally. Did surgeons want people they had operated on to come over for dinner? Did dentists say to their patients, "After I drill one more tooth, come over to my house, and I'll get out my brandy?"

The problem had been that everyone was either her customer, or everyone was her customer potentially. She tried to remember the last time someone had come into her house. She couldn't remember. "Twilight," said Guida, out loud, "and getting dimmer by the second."

Or maybe it was Mr. Dunfee who had spoken, and she happened to tune in her ears to him for those words. She couldn't tell. She didn't care. She didn't even mind it that the rock she was on was far from flat or smooth. It wasn't a seat-like slab of granite. It was jagged and bumpy, with strange little stony, pointed protrusions.

She wasn't thinking about what her backside would feel like later, and she wasn't wondering if her stockings had any more rips, or if, for days and days and days, she'd be picking bits of pebbles from her skirt.

She was watching the old man's face and she was watching the air and she was thinking about a basic fact.

She was wondering if there was anyone who ever lived, in all of time, who never once pictured themselves, at the backs of their eyes, in a picture of what they'll look like when they are dead. It wouldn't matter if they lived in a house, or a cave, or a cheap little hut in the woods somewhere, with a roof on their heads of just animal skins and some sticks to prop them up.

Well, didn't everyone, from the beginning of time, have pictures come into their heads—maybe in dreams, or maybe wide awake, in daylight—of themselves lying flat on their backs, in a big dark box or a hole, quite dead? And didn't everyone also wonder—maybe just once, or maybe often—how good it would feel to just drop what they happen to be doing, and go off on their own somewhere—somewhere dark—and get it over with, seeing as how it's going to happen anyway?

Of course everyone had these thoughts. Who could be a normal human being and never have them?

Maybe it didn't have to be an actual picture. Maybe you had to reach a certain age before it happens. Maybe, sometimes, it was a sudden, icy sense that came over you out of nowhere, as real as when a cloud blocks the sun.

Then you'd look all around, and you would see that, although nothing looked changed, something inside you was very different. You'd look up at a cloud, or at foggy night air, and you'd understand the basic law of what would happen: there would always be clouds in the sky, and there would always be fog, but there would not always be you.

There was a jingle long ago on the radio for a powdered household cleanser called Mrs. Shine-O.

It hadn't lasted very long—not the ad and not the cleanser—but Guida remembered it well. The jingle said nothing about the powers of the soap, or the benefits of mixing it in water, or ways in which it surpassed other products. It went,

> *Oh, I am Mrs. Shine-O,*
> *Oh, I am Mrs. Shine-O,*
> *Oh, I am Mrs. Shine-O,*
> *You can count on me.*

It wasn't just a careless little ditty: the tune was the saddest piece of music, Guida felt, that had ever been played in a commercial. There was only one instrument and it was a flute, as if a flute had been invited to a requiem.

The singer was an alto. Her voice came to Guida like a voice from the bottom of a cave, not a voice on the radio. If you bought that cleanser, would you also be buying the alto, the flute? No, it was only a commercial. All that came out of a box of Mrs. Shine-O was powder.

"I feel like Mrs. Shine-O," Guida said to herself.

The line between twilight and night was like a pole through the center of the sky. The top of the pole was where north was. When the last gray shadows flickered out, darkness opened up like a black umbrella.

The dark air smelled like autumn, like dirt, like leaves, and so did Mr. Dunfee. It wasn't fair that she couldn't remember if he'd been her customer before. As hard as she tried, she remembered nothing about him except his face and his name.

He must have had some kind of a job. He was a strong, able-bodied man, and his hands were the hands of someone who had never been idle. As coarse as his skin was, his hands had a sort of elegance, or a suppleness, and it didn't seem like this was something he'd acquired from his employers.

He must have been living away from home for a long time. And out here, in the middle of nowhere, in all these trees! As a gardener, as a servant, keeping everything tidy!

She would have to try harder to remember Harold Dunfee. She wished she'd paid attention to his words, but nothing could be done about the fact that many of the words went into her ears like words in a different language, and all she heard were the tones, the notes.

She still was sitting on the rock. "Try harder," she said to herself. "Don't just sit here remembering Mrs. Shine-O."

Mr. Dunfee smelled like autumn and dirt and leaves.

Guida remembered what autumn had smelled like back in town when people raked leaves into piles, and burned them to cinders in long, slow fires in front of their houses, on sidewalks, or in the gutters of roads. Smoke curled up from those fires like smoke from an offering, with its own smell of leafy, twiggy incense.

It was as good as the smell of something cooking.

She remembered that, when she was a girl, she used to stand by burning leaves and look straight up north at evening twilight, and imagine that a one-eyed god—any god, it didn't matter what type of god—was always there.

The one eye, she had imagined, was exactly in the center of the sky, always obscured, but never quite all the way closed. No one ever saw it. You just had to believe that it was there.

That was the trick of it. You just had to believe, and whatever it saw, so could you. You just had to believe you were lucky enough to do things that were astonishing.

Sixteen

"I may not be religious," Mr. Dunfee said, "but if I end up sending myself to the devil as the last thing on earth I choose to do, that's something I want to know about ahead of time, Signora, if you don't mind."

Guida waited a long time before she spoke, and when she did at last, it was to Tara. What she said was not what Tara had expected.

Tara had to wonder if perhaps she hadn't noticed that Mr. Dunfee, in spite of the brightness in his eyes and the smooth, velvety, singsong way he worked his tongue around words, was very, very depressed.

Guida did not seem to care that he was asking her for her opinion on whether or not he'd go to hell.

"Harold, in his day, when I knew of him back in town," said Guida, "was an artist."

"Signora. You remember." Mr. Dunfee blushed and accepted the compliment by putting his unattractive plaid cap back on his head—he'd been holding it all along in his hands—and quickly taking it off again.

He looked at Tara for the first time and said, "How old are you, anyway?"

Already Tara was finished with thinking about ages. If other people wanted to be obsessed with people's ages, in a close-minded, simplistic, narrow-minded way, as if that's what really mattered, ages, well, let them all be obsessed—Mr. Dunfee, her parents, the partners, Tommy, everyone. She was completely clear in her mind, and it wasn't only because she'd already worked out the math on the difference between twenty-four and fifty-three.

OK, she thought, there were an awful lot of numbers in between, but she knew, when you come right down to it, all of the time in someone's life, is divided into four main parts, just like a clock or a compass.

There were four main categories of ages: you were a baby; you were a child, which also included being a teenager; then you were a grown-up; then you were old. Tara pictured this. Mr. Dunfee was old. She and Guida, together, were in the third category.

They totally had it in common that both of them were grown-ups.

Tara said to Mr. Dunfee, "I'm older than I look. I'm practically going to be thirty."

"Thirty, eh?" said Mr. Dunfee. She thought he was mocking her, but he wasn't. "Then you're old enough to know I never was sorry I stole cars."

He stole *cars?*

"What I see for you first, Mr. Dunfee, has more to do with the next few hours, than later on in a hole by yourself, in case you still might be inclined in that direction," said Guida. "I can see that first, you might need to have something to do that perhaps would give you the chance to use your powers." She paused, then added, "I mean, your skill."

He swallowed so deeply, Tara could hear it. He looked at Guida with hopeful eyes. "Which skill would that be?"

"It would be," said Guida, "you might want to have a talk with this girl about a job."

"This girl?"

"This girl."

"Signora," said Mr. Dunfee, "for what kind of a job exactly?"

"It's a little red car with a large, unusual, eye-catching sign on it," said Guida.

"And what would need to be done to it?"

"It would need," said Guida, "to be rescued from the parking lot of a motel. In fact, it would need to be rescued from under the noses of some people who might be watching it very closely."

"Rescued," said Mr. Dunfee. "I like that."

He looked like someone who'd been very, very hungry, and someone else had dangled in front of his eyes some wonderful bit of food—and just as he feared they would take it away, it was his, and he was grabbing at it. Tara had never seen anyone before pass over so quickly from misery to joy. It felt good to be looking at Mr. Dunfee.

He started wringing his cap in his old brown hands, as if that were the only way he could think of to contain his excitement. He said to Guida, in almost a whisper, "She fences cars?"

"I wish! All I can do is find jobs!" cried Tara.

Guida took off her glasses and put them in her purse and patted Mr. Dunfee on the shoulder. Did that mean the seeing was over? Was that really a seeing?

"I think I have a pen somewhere," said Mr. Dunfee. "I will carefully write down the address as I wouldn't expect you to trust the memory of an old man, not that I'm saying I have problems with my memory."

He patted his pockets. Tara whispered to Guida, "Was that a seeing?"

"I'm not sure," whispered Guida.

"Why not? Because he's not paying you?"

"No," whispered Guida, "it's not the money."

"Because it's outdoors?"

"Outdoors wouldn't matter."

THE WHITE PALAZZO

"Because it happened accidentally? He didn't have an appointment? He just was here?"

Guida shook her head.

Tara said, "Because you haven't got your, you know, extra eye?"

"I don't know. To tell you the truth, I just don't know. Maybe it was a seeing. I'll have to figure that out later."

"Later when?"

"Tara, I don't know."

"Well, I don't care if you've got the eye or not, I'm calling it a seeing." Then she said, "Guida! I watched you do a seeing!"

Guida smiled at her. It was a different sort of smile from all the different ones Tara had seen on her so far, including the one that had come after Tara had kissed her, as she'd climbed out from the back of the van.

This time, Guida drew her lips way back and wide open, so her teeth and gums showed. There were hooks in there. Janey had got it right; some of those teeth were definitely artificial.

Tara felt grateful that she had discovered this fact with her eyes, instead of finding it out the hard way, with her tongue. Maybe older people, like Guida, needed to have a rule about the first time they're kissed by someone. "Don't open your mouth until you get to know the person who's kissing you a lot, lot better," was probably how it went.

"Excuse me for the hurry, but can I go now?" said Mr. Dunfee. He didn't have a car of his own and he didn't even have a driver's license, but there was a bus that went down through the valley and the last one was about to leave. Please, where was he supposed to be going?

He'd found a pen in one of his pockets. He wrote the name and address of the Hathaway on the back of his hand.

Tara watched him to make sure he spelled it correctly. He asked, "Would this be a foreign job or an American?"

"It's a Mustang," said Guida.

"Does it have an alarm?"

Guida looked at Tara. Tara shook her head, and Guida said to Mr. Dunfee, "I think you'll have to be careful with this. The car we're talking about, as it happens, was reported as being stolen." Then she said, "Don't ask why. Just be very, very careful."

"I know the back roads like my own bones," said Mr. Dunfee. "The mounties on their horses out here, they don't know half about the roads as I do. To be worried about police, Signora, is something we do not need to do."

Then he was gone. Tara had turned for just an instant to look over her shoulder at the wavy, yellow-white lights of the cottage, and he was gone. One minute he was standing beside her so closely, she could smell the mud on his clothes and his sweat and a scent of old tobacco. The next minute, when she looked back, he had vanished. There wasn't even a sound of leaves underfoot in the distance, although he had to cross through the woods behind the cottage to get to the main road for his bus.

"Guida!" cried Tara. "My car! He doesn't know where to bring it if he gets it! He doesn't know anything!"

"Don't worry," said Guida. "He's always had a reputation for being dependable. He'll know what to do."

"But he took off! I got my hopes up about getting back my car and he took off!"

"You can still have your hopes up."

"Ha!" said Tara.

Some seeing! Everything that had just gone on with Mr. Dunfee, Tara now saw, had gone very, very badly, in spite of the joy on his face, and Guida was standing there, smiling from ear to ear with her hooks showing plainly, and acting as if she were telling herself, "That went great."

The glee that Tara had felt at the thought of getting back her car went out like a snuffed-out candle. Who was the odd man, anyway? How had he disappeared so fast?

And look at the way he was dressed. He was just like a picture of Rumpelstiltskin, come to life from out of a fairy tale. Maybe below the surface of his golden-tongued words and his misery, he was as evil-hearted as that hunchback dwarf Rumpelstiltskin—who could trust anyone?

It was preposterous to think a man who'd come out of nowhere would be able to take care of the one thing she needed—she missed her car! She felt that her heart was sinking. How could he grant her what she wanted? How could she get her hopes up? Guida couldn't see into the future!

"Stupid eye," thought Tara. "Stupid, stupid, stupid eye."

What would happen to her car?

She pictured it in the Hathaway parking lot. The teenage boy from the sign shop had probably parked it next to Guida's rental. That very moment, Tara imagined, her mother, her father, Tommy, Ax, Bone, Wee, and Robocop, in a huddle, were looking at her name on the roof. They were probably not admiring her sign.

"My poor little hostage of a car," thought Tara. Where was Janey, anyway? How long could it take to drive back for stupid vases?

The mild, balmy, soft autumn air of daylight was gone. It was almost as cold as if winter had started already. Her skin prickled with goosebumps. There was only a very slight wind but it cut to her skin as if her clothes were as flimsy as rags.

Would Janey really come back?

She was sick of stupid Janey. She was hungry; she was cold. Her pockets were empty. She had no idea where she was on an actual point on a map; she had no wallet, no coat, no anything.

It had been a long day and it looked like it was about to get longer. She was sick of not having her car.

She was sick of looking at the cottage. She was sick of being west. She was sick of houses in the middle of nowhere, and hills that were not the hills of home, and she was sick of looking at really, really big trees. As beautiful as the hemlocks were in daylight and dusk, they were not attractive in the dark. Those long-armed, long-fingered branches were like something she might see in a nightmare.

No wonder Mr. Dunfee imagined himself in a hole with a bottle. He was old, no one loved him, he hated his own heart. Did this happen to everyone, once you reached a certain age?

Tara tried to imagine Guida *old*. This could happen: "I'm going out now to dig myself a hole now," Guida could say.

She would have taken out her teeth. She would have put on a sweater. She would have shrunk, as old people always do. She would have resembled Mr. Dunfee very closely—a female Mr. Dunfee, hating her own heart because it wouldn't stop beating. What was the use of a beating heart, if the only person who cared if it was still ticking was yourself?

"I'm going to the hardware store for a shovel," she would say, and Tara might answer, "I'll drive you! I'll pay for it!" She could picture herself getting so fed up with Guida, she'd want to dig the hole herself.

Would she really go off to the hardware store to buy a shovel? What if she didn't give any warning? Which direction was the hardware store from her house?

It was north. First she'd go north, then what? Tara imagined herself trying to track Guida down. Where would she dig the hole? Not in any woods like Mr. Dunfee. Not in her yard, either, where her neighbors would be watching.

"White Cliffs Hill," thought Tara.

She could picture Guida plodding up White Cliffs Hill at the age of eighty with a shovel on her shoulder like Jesus' cross, and being over-dramatic about it, too: her hair would be wild, her sweater would be buttoned all wrong, she'd look like she was homeless. Probably if Tara helped her dig the hole, she would then have to get into it, too.

No way was she letting Guida lie around in one by herself, like someone who wasn't loved. "Just what I need," Tara thought. What if she wanted to be buried at White Cliffs?

What if someone else had bought the land, what if there was going to be another r - - - - - - - - -? Tara could picture that, too. It would be just like Guida to put "bury me at White Cliffs, if I haven't done so already," in her will.

Tara sighed. "Maybe I'll have to buy the whole hill," she said to herself.

She thought of her pillowcase back at the Hathaway. She thought of what was in her savings account, her checking account. She thought about what it had felt like walking in the sunlight on the road to the diner, and not wanting a hole to open up at Guida's feet, just like that, a hole through the center of the earth. A crevasse.

She wished all over again that Guida still had her eye. She wished Guida knew what she was thinking.

Guida took hold of her arm. "Tara," said Guida. "Listen."

Over by the cottage, a horn was being blown—it must have been Janey, although it sounded too polite and subdued for the van.

Guida clutched at Tara and pulled her along behind her, out of the woods and into the clearing and into the driveway by the side of the old stone cottage. The person in the shadows who was waiting for them was Janey, all right. Tara could make out her shape, her cap.

But it wasn't the van. It was Guida's rented Buick. The keys were jiggling in Janey's hand.

The rented Buick!

"I got it just fine!" cried Janey. "I went to the motel and called up my husband and he brought over the stupid vases and it went great, just like you said! I told my sister to tell everyone that I worked for the rental car place, like I was doing a repo job! Signora! No one knows you were ever there! Not even the detective!"

"Detective," said Guida, like Janey's echo.

"I almost forgot about him!" cried Janey.

She turned to Tara. "Your bosses hired a private eye from Boston. He's there with them now. I think he just showed up to make sure they pay him. He's big and he looks like Charlton Heston. He looks like an ad for the NRA. My sister says he wanted to kick in the door of your room to see if you were in there but he didn't, because he didn't want to spend his money on another door."

"Thank you," said Guida, to Janey.

"I just acted like everything was pure business! I left the van at the motel with my husband! He's on his way home! You can drop me off at home!"

"Guida?" said Tara. "Don't tell me you hired Janey to steal this rental."

"I gave her the keys," said Guida.

Tara hoped that her astonishment wasn't showing. She hoped that it seemed as if she didn't feel—feel what? Left out? Tricked? Was that what she felt, tricked?

"It was right in front of your eyes," Guida added. "It was just before I started talking with Harold. Maybe you were thinking about something else. You were standing right there and I handed Janey the keys and asked her to please get my rental on the way to getting the vases, and off she went, and here she is."

It was true, of course it would have to be true—everything Guida said seemed so true. Was it? Everything?

"They want to take you back with them so you can get married," said Janey. "But everything went perfect. The car handled fantastic and I never would have thought I'd praise a Buick. And you should see my sister and Mopey! Eight rented rooms! They all checked in, even the detective! They think you're walking in the door any second! My sister and Mopey said to tell you, 'Tara, way to go! Stay away!'"

"I am not," said Tara, "getting married."

"That's just what I used to say," said Janey. "I went around for two years saying 'I'm never getting married,' and I think my husband drugged me. I went into this walking, talking coma. When I finally snapped out of it, I had a wedding ring on, and I was a partner in a floral business, neither of which I would have done if I wasn't drugged, so, I know how you feel."

"But I made up my mind!" cried Tara.

"Everyone's still waiting for you to show up and face the music," said Janey. "Except the detective. He just wants to get some sleep before he goes home."

That sounded like something the partners would say: face the music.

And what type of music would that be? It would be something she'd put her hands on her ears to block out, that was what.

Was she supposed to be flattered that the partners paid money for a detective? What if he'd got there before Guida? Oh no! What if there were no Guida?

Oh no! Did she have to tell Guida she was sorry for thinking they had all turned up at the motel because Guida had led them there? How many hours had gone by since she'd promised Guida she'd never give her a reason again to have to forgive her? Not many hours had gone by, even though it felt like a lot.

"I have to tell you," said Janey. A worried look appeared on her face. "It's none of my business if your parents have problems with their marriage, but they checked into separate rooms."

"Who's paying?" said Tara.

"Your bosses are putting it all on a credit card."

"Which rooms are my parents in?"

"Lime and grape," said Janey.

Lime and grape were side by side. This was a good sign. "They would think it was a luxury to sleep apart from each other and have their own bathrooms. Their marriage is great," said Tara.

"Did they eat?" said Guida.

"They ordered pizza," said Janey. "Plus they bought four liters of Pepsi and a gallon of really good, really expensive Puerto Rican rum. And my sister's going out to the video store in case there's nothing to watch on cable. And the guy she's marrying already took a shower, and he shaved, too, not that he needed it, and he borrowed a ton of Old Spice from Mopey, and he is hanging out at the counter right now so he's the first thing she sees when she walks in."

"But I'm not getting married to him!" cried Tara.

The man in the cottage called out from one of the windows, "Thanks for the delivery and going back for the vases but please, will you please go away?"

Janey got into the back of the Buick, then leaned out the door and tossed the keys to Guida. But quickly, lightly, Tara jumped forward and caught them neatly.

"I'm driving," she said.

Guida looked over at her with eyebrows raised, and Tara thought she'd point out to her the fact that the insurance on the rental was just for herself: letting Tara drive would be illegal. Or she'd tell her to be careful about handling the Buick, which, compared to what Tara was used to, would be like trying to drive an ox, even though Janey had liked it.

But Guida just said, "All right."

"Guida? Do I have to tell you I'm sorry because I said everyone must have followed you to me, from town? If you want me to, I will, but I won't really mean it, because how was I supposed to know they'd get a detective?"

"It's not a sorry-for thing. You were just being logical."

"No one ever said that to me before," said Tara.

The car keys felt good in Tara's hand. "I was wondering," she said, "where we should go."

The word came out so easily. "We." Was this all right, that it came to her so easily? Was it abnormal?

"I was wondering the same thing," said Guida.

"Let's go!" cried Janey, from the car.

"But everything I have is back at the Hathaway," said Tara.

"Well, not everything." Guida didn't point to herself as she said this, but Tara had the feeling that she did.

"Well, if you're going to tell me to drive back there and face the music," said Tara, "you don't have to bother because, I already know I'm not facing it, at least, not tonight, and if you think I'm sadistic as a daughter, and I'm totally selfish, you can think so if you want to. I don't care what you think. If you think I don't know what I'm doing, you can think that, too, but you'd be totally, totally wrong."

"It wouldn't be the first time," said Guida.

"Stop talking!" cried Janey. She banged both hands on the back seat of the Buick, as if she were playing a bongo.

Where were they supposed to go? To another motel? Stay at Janey's for supper? And watch Janey and her husband make floral arrangements for someone's retirement, or a funeral? Sit around with them, and stick colored, ugly carnations into styrofoam balls?

Go hide somewhere, like outlaws? Hide where? Go out to the mall and have supper at the food court? Then what? Buy a few things? Underwear? One change of clothes, for tomorrow? Tooth-brushes, toothpaste, those fizzy blue tablets for false teeth?

"Tara," said Guida. "Seeing as how all those people from home are out here, waiting for you, maybe you ought to drive home."

"I have to pee," called out Janey. "If you don't stop talking and get into this car, I'll get out and pee in these people's front yard."

Tara looked at Guida. "You want to go *home?*"

"I do."

"Home where?"

"To my house," said Guida.

"Right now?"

"Right now."

"For the night, do you mean, or for good?"

"Maybe," said Guida, "they can mean the same thing."

Seventeen

They dropped off Janey; the van was in the driveway.

She lived in a Cape at the end of another, long country road; the house doubled as their floral business. The greenhouses on either side were like long, wide igloos, with plastic, transparent walls.

The front yard had been landscaped. Instead of a lawn there were terraced layers of empty flower beds, and the dirt was covered with whatever that powdery white stuff was that gardeners put on dirt for the winter. Each layer was lined at the edges with rows and rows of perfectly smooth white pebbles, like oversized bits of gravel, and in the headlights of the Buick, and the light from Janey's porch, it looked as if snow had been falling.

"You've been very, very kind, and thank you for offering me a job, too, even though I would be unsuitable," said Guida.

Janey jumped out of the car and rushed over to her husband as if she'd been separated from him for a year.

Matt Hathaway had come out from one of the greenhouses. He was lanky and tall, and his jacket was slung back on his shoulders, wide open. Under it was a white T-shirt. He wore his jeans down low on his hips. "Hi, Runaway," he called out. He was waving to her at the same time he was hugging Janey.

"I'm doing it again!" cried Tara.

"Snow," said Guida.

She looked at the terraces, then pointed to Janey's husband. His jacket was a bright yellow rubber windbreaker, and the black rubber boots on his feet—he'd been watering plants in the greenhouse—went up his legs as high as fishermen's waders, and they looked wet.

"It looks like Alaska," said Guida.

"It's those greenhouses and all that white stuff and rocks," said Tara.

"He looks like a fisherman," said Guida. She was still pointing to Matt. "I know a salmon fisherman from Alaska who looks just like him."

"You want to come in?" Matt called out.

"No!" cried Tara.

She backed out of the driveway and it was a good thing it was wide and there was nothing to hit. Driving the Buick was not like driving an ox, it was worse. It was like trying to drive a stupid, jumbo boat.

Knows a salmon fisherman *how?*

By the time Tara felt she could relax a little at the wheel and look over at Guida, who was very, very quiet, they were still on back roads, about ten miles from the highway. Quiet why? Because she was thinking about her fisherman? Where was he now? Was he alive?

She had not believed Guida about having a truck. If she drove to Guida's house, would she find one in Guida's driveway? The pickup of a fisherman, and then the fisherman himself, bounding out, just like Matt?

Into his arms would rush Guida. He'd think Tara was a taxi driver, or part-time temping as Guida's chauffeur. He'd come over to her. "Did Guida Santucci, who I'm going to make love to, as soon as I can get her alone, remember to give you a tip?"

He probably didn't live with Guida, but he would act as if he did. Maybe he came down from Gloucester, or up from Cape Cod, for the weekend. This was the weekend. He was probably in her kitchen making dinner. He was probably making salmon.

Tara had placed clients in a fish-processing plant in Rhode Island—they'd had to take a bus that left town before dawn—but she couldn't remember anything they'd told her about the guys who worked the boats. They had only wanted to tell her that people who handle fish never, ever want to eat it. But maybe they meant fish *sticks*. That was what they made in the plant.

"Darling, I am broiling you a salmon." And what would Guida answer? "Darling, I had a huge, huge lunch, at a very rural diner, but it's been a long day, and I'm starving"?

When he kissed her, did she like it, or just put up with it? He was probably grizzly. He was probably extremely hairy. He was probably the kind of man who had hair across his shoulders, and in his ears. He probably didn't use cologne. He probably smelled like fish. He probably drank a lot, too. He probably had calluses all over his hands. The skin of his fingers would feel like sandpaper. Where did he put those fingers? How could she let him near her?

"Guida?" said Tara.

In the glow of the dashboard, which had an instrument panel like something on a jet, if the jet was being flown by someone who did not have a brain, Tara saw that Guida had fallen asleep. Again! She'd put her head against the headrest, and that was that. She was not snoring.

"Great," thought Tara. "Now she wants to dream about him."

The gas tank was full. They wouldn't have to stop for gas. Maybe there wasn't a man. Maybe, imagining a man was like Guida imagining a black Ford truck in her own driveway. Why had she made it up about owning a truck, had she wanted to seem impressive? That would be forgivable, Tara felt.

But what about everything else?

A terrible thought had been forming in the back of Tara's mind, and now that she was out on the open road, with no one to talk to, it came up to the surface with a jarring, awful leap, and blocked out everything else. It was a hundred times harder to cope with than the blister of remorse about her parents.

The nervousness she had felt all those weeks ago—driving in the other direction; driving west into twilight and fog, toward the western hills, alone, on the day of the f- - -, when she'd bolted, because that was what she had done, she had bolted, like a horse—well, all of that was nothing compared to the panic that was gathering up inside her right now. It was worse than worrying about whether or not someone she didn't want to fall into crevasses, fell into one. A cold feeling came over her. It was the same as if she were back in the road at the bottom of White Cliffs Hill, being robbed three times.

Was this the fourth? Was she wrong about robberies only happening in threes? Was that just a superstition? Was there no such thing as being immune to what it's like when you've been tricked, and by the very last person you would ever expect to have tricked you? Tricked was the same as robbed. Tricked was another way to say "broke my heart," which always sounded so unbelievable, as if a heart were a plate or a glass.

She wasn't thinking, "I am having second thoughts about Guida Santucci." She wasn't thinking, exactly, "Here I go again, just like when Tommy said he knew what I was talking about when I told him about my compass."

She was thinking very clearly, though. She was thinking about Guida's description in the diner of what sunrise was like through the White Cliffs windows, in the days just before the Gallaghers took it over and turned it into a r- - - - - - - - - -.

Tara knew that the description had been accurate. Hadn't she been there herself? She knew exactly what the light was like in the big main banquet room first thing in the morning, because she'd been there to talk about her wedding with the janitor who opened up for the deliveries, and the baker who came in at five to start the breads, rolls, and turnovers.

She knew what the light was like at noon, at three, and in the evening. How could anyone put into words what the light was like at White Cliffs, when they hadn't seen it?

Guida wouldn't have made it up about the two words, "White Cliffs," and what it felt like to hear them in the voice of the very young nun. Would she make it all up? Was White Cliffs like Major's grave? Was the story of how she got her extra eye *payback?*

"I should have known," thought Tara. "She is not to be trusted, and she is also vindictive."

The highway stretched out in front of her, lit up with lights of cars, lit up with strings of streetlights, all running together as if someone were pouring out white and red and yellow lights from one bucket, or one hose. She had to be careful.

No way was she going to let herself give in to any panic and run the car off the road into a ditch, and there'd she be with Guida, upside down, with the Buick wheels spinning in the air and Massachusetts State Troopers shining flashlights in their eyes, and nudging each other on the hips where their guns were, and asking, "Now, what have you two ladies been doing together, exactly?"

She wasn't feeling any panic!

East, they were going. East like the rising sun, although it felt as if sunrise would be a long, long time away. How could she have thought she knew what she was doing? What was wrong with her, was she in shock? Had she been doing things she didn't know about, as if acting behind her own back?

Maybe this was how it felt to be someone who suffered from the disorder of having multiple personalities; maybe it was psychological. Tara tried to remember the different disorders she'd read about in the textbook for the night school class she never took. She'd kept the book. Maybe the girl who had jumped out at Guida and caught her car keys—"I'm driving"—was another Tara entirely, and so was the girl who had sat in the diner, wishing that the big table between Guida and herself would crumple like a table made of paper.

She would have to be polite to Guida when the time came to say good-bye to her. "I wasn't myself when you walked into the Hathaway and found me. Bye, now, and thanks for telling me about your eye, if you really do have one."

Her thoughts, she would say, had not been her own; it was all just a terrible, embarrassing disorder. She pictured herself entering the valley, entering town, and driving down White Cliffs Hill Road to Guida's house, and dropping her off like a taxi driver, even though they were in Guida's car. Would White Cliffs Hill be invisible in the darkness? It would have to be. There would be no lights.

"Bye now," she would say. That would be herself, the genuine Tara, and she would explain very carefully what had happened. She'd speak to Guida as "Signora," as if they had never met. "Something you didn't know about me is that I have multiple personalities, Signora," she would say. "The girl who kissed you wasn't me. Neither was the girl who's been looking at you in a certain way. The girl who made it up about Major also wasn't me, and neither was the one who got up from the table with you at the diner."

"Sarah," she thought. She'd have to give names to her personalities, like in *Sybil,* except that hers, she decided, would be girls. Weren't two of Sybil's personalities guys? Oh no! Was one of hers a guy already, Homer Simpson?

         THE WHITE PALAZZO

"Great," thought Tara. "Tara, Sarah, and Farrah, like in Farrah Fawcett. And then Homer."

That was as far as she got in trying to blame everything that had happened to her today on phantom personalities. It didn't do any good. She had no one to blame except herself. There was only her same old self, Tara Barlow.

All she could do was picture Guida across the table from her in the diner. How many hours had they sat there, with Guida talking and talking? She didn't know. She couldn't remember the last time she'd seen a clock. From the moment Guida walked in the door of the Hathaway, there weren't minutes or hours. There was the daylight of morning, the daylight of afternoon, the dusk, and now the night.

It was as if Guida had brought her outside of measured time. Tara didn't have a watch on. Why would she have put on a watch? All she'd planned to do today was wait for the weekend to pass by, so Monday would come, and she could get her car back from the sign shop. "We're going out for groceries and then we're going to the bank to put off a few more bills. Mind the desk for us," the Hathaways had said, as if anyone would really check in, as if they weren't one step away from foreclosure.

They had thought it was funny that she was playing the role of one of her own clients. "Today you're our own private temp, Tara," they had said. The money for the groceries had come from what Tara had paid them for her room.

Yes, if she wanted to stay there and live with them forever, she could do it, they wouldn't mind. No, they didn't want Tara to find them different jobs; they just wanted to hang onto their motel. They didn't care how inept they were, and they didn't care that they had picked the wrong place for a motel.

"Something will happen for the good," they kept saying. "We

live from loan to loan." And they wouldn't declare themselves bankrupt. As they'd put it themselves, that would mean "throwing in the towel." They couldn't throw in a towel. They didn't own one. The towels in every room were mortgaged, too.

She had sat on a stool behind the counter. There was something about the stillness of all those empty rooms that made her happy, which she felt was very strange.

Why should she have been happy at the edge of a big stretch of woods, near a rundown, depressed, western town, on a road that was practically in the middle of nowhere, with nothing to look at but an empty parking lot and a field of thorny, wild apple trees? She didn't know. She didn't know a way to say to herself, "Even though everyone back home will think I'm selfish and completely irresponsible, I am fine."

And then there was Guida. She'd looked up, and Guida was standing in front of her, in her Republican-looking skirt and expensive, tailored blouse.

"Tara Barlow," she had said. "You look normal."

Then they went out to look at Major's grave.

And then she talked about being fat, being Catholic, the rain, her school, the crippled boy, the thug of a nun who had hit her, and the old, fat Italian tailor who was a witch. And then the trip to the white palazzo and the flute of the younger nun's voice saying those words in English, "White Cliffs," and the light, and the eye that stood up inside her like something just born, oh *no!* What if it was really just a story like Major's grave?

Or, if not a story, a parable. Just because Guida had told her that she wasn't a Catholic any more didn't mean she wasn't still a Catholic. Tara had known Catholics on Johnson Street, and every one of her Mexican clients was one, and so were two of the partners, Ax and Wee. Catholics liked parables.

Parables were stories about things that never take place in reality. They were not to be believed, although once, a Mexican who temped in the post office—he called himself Chay; that was all, Chay—had told her an extraordinary story—a parable—about a thirteen-year-old girl from South America who was living, illegally, in the valley.

The girl had never done anything miraculous before, and she never did again, but one day, a man from Immigration showed up at her family's door, and she calmly took charge. She said to her mother and father, who were panicking, "Don't worry. I'm completely dependable. I'm putting a cloak of invisibility on us."

She waved her arms in the air and said something in Spanish, and then everyone peeked out the windows at the Immigration man, who was standing there pointing his finger at nothing. He was standing there as if wondering, "Why do I think I rang a doorbell, when there's no bell, there's not even a house?" Then he walked away, shaking his head and saying, "I need a drink."

Tara had not believed Chay's story until she happened to have found herself in the family's neighborhood one afternoon. She'd gone to their house and said, "I know Chay," and they told her that it was true. She had ended up recruiting the girl's mother for a temp job with the telephone company, then later as a door-to-door Census Bureau worker, which she'd been great at.

If Guida's story was a parable, a parable about what? Was she simply trying to put herself in a positive light, as anyone would do, when you are sitting across a table from someone you perhaps are falling in love with, and they're sitting there, looking at you, and maybe, they're doing the same thing?

Oh no! What about that tailor?

That was an aspect of Guida's story that could be checked. All Tara had to do was pick up a phone and call the town clerk—her name was Nancy Doherty. Tara had put lots of temps in her office; she could call her at home. "Check on a fat Italian tailor from a long time ago who everyone said was a witch." It would also be easy to check on the Grayfrocks. The rest of it was uncertain.

If it was a parable, what about the crippled boy? Wouldn't Guida have put in a little more? Wouldn't she have said, "The day after I talked to him in the hallway, when I felt that I was in two places at once, he got up and started walking around, completely healed?"

Maybe not. Maybe she was being modest, as if to emphasize a quality of hers that Tara should notice.

What about that light?

And she wondered, which thing would be worse—if Guida lied about a man who was her lover, or if she lied about getting her eye?

Well, if a man was at her house after all, there was only one thing to be done. There wouldn't have to be a scene about it. It wasn't as if she'd do something immature and gloat about it and rub it in, saying, "I'm sorry to tell you this, but you've just been replaced, and by a *girl.*"

The man would have to leave and never come back; that was simple. But what if there was no such thing as that eye?

Hadn't she sat down with the odd little man and pretended that she was giving him a seeing? She was Guida Santucci! She told fortunes! She wasn't like other people! Everyone knew who she was!

It was all falling into place in Tara's mind. It embarrassed her to think how easily she'd fallen for Guida, and that was the only way to describe it; she had *fallen.* All along, back on the road to the diner, when she was watching for crevasses for Guida not to fall into, she should have been watching out for herself.

She was down in a hole, all right. She was driving across Massachusetts in the dark, with lights rushing by her like lights that were made of colored water, like something poured out of a hose, and she was cold inside and hollow, and all along, at the same time, she was way down a hole.

She knew she wasn't starting to cry, because if she were, it would have to come hard, it would have to break out of her like a cloudburst, she felt, not in teary little trickles.

What if, what if, what if, what if? What if there was no such thing as that eye? What if Guida Santucci was just the same as other people?

She couldn't believe she had let herself be seduced. That was what it was, wasn't it, seduced? Like someone on a television talk show pouring their heart out because of things that were damaged in them, because of things someone told them that weren't true? It would simply be a basic sob story, wouldn't it, like one million others, in an average, normal way, and everyone could see it on a talk show?

"Oh, they told me this, they told me that, they were so romantic to me, they made me feel like I never felt before, and my heart was a glass and they broke it," and the people in the talk-show audience are clucking their tongues without sympathy, saying, "Girl, you are so pathetic."

"Please don't turn out to be a liar," Tara was thinking. "Please don't be a liar when you look at me the way you do. Please don't be a liar when you're talking about something important. Please don't be a liar when you say the things to me that you've been saying."

Was that four things? It was.

"Guida," she said. "Wake up."

"I'm awake," said Guida. Then she said, "Why are you turning on the windshield wipers?"

"Sorry, I was just trying to figure out the controls. It's not like I ever drove this kind of car before." Tara turned off the wipers. She pretended to fiddle with the other knobs. She could not believe she had thought it had started raining.

"I was just thinking," Guida said, "how you never look in the rearview mirror. How can you drive a car and never look at what's behind you?"

"Don't tell me how to drive."

"It was just a suggestion."

Tara gripped the wheel a little harder, and pressed her foot harder on the gas. Guida said, "I'm worried about Mr. Dunfee. I'm worried about his heart."

"His heart is great. That's what he said, in case you weren't listening."

"I listened," said Guida. "But you never know, when someone's that old, how much they can take."

"How much what?"

"Oh, excitement," said Guida.

What kind of excitement? Mr. Dunfee was elderly, weary, and depressed. He looked like an evil dwarf hunchback in a fairy tale.

"He's probably an alcoholic," said Tara. "And he's also probably crazy, so don't make up stories about how I'm getting back my car from a car thief. Did you see the way he was dressed?"

What if there was no such thing as that eye? What if it weren't true that, after the f - - -, it stopped working, it curled up and shut its lid, perhaps for good? That was what Tara had believed, like a fact. Why should she have believed this? What if it was never there at all?

"I could test her," thought Tara. She tried to think of a test to give Guida, right now, to prove everything, one way or another.

Guida said, "Tara?"

"What!" Tara jumped in her seat. Her hand went up to her eyes to wipe away the tears that were there, as if it were working on its own, quite without her.

"Stupid hand, stupid body, stupid eyes, stupid everything,"

thought Tara. She couldn't believe she couldn't think of a test to give Guida. She couldn't believe she had gotten herself in this situation. She couldn't believe she had kissed a woman, and *liked* it.

Guida said, "Do you never look in rearview mirrors, or are you only not doing it now?"

"None of your business."

Tara watched the speedometer go eighty, eighty-five. She could not believe what a hurry she was in to get back to town—to do what? Track down the different elements of Guida's story? Get away from Guida for forever? Go home by herself to Johnson Street, and not spend even one second wondering what Guida was doing on White Cliffs Hill Road?

Tara pictured herself walking toward her apartment block as if she never had left it: no one would be at home. "This has been a very, very strange day," she would say to the sofa. "Now I am back to myself." She'd touch the chairs, she'd look around with contentment. "It was just like *The Wizard of Oz,*" she might say, to a lamp. She'd act just like Dorothy when she woke up in her bed in Kansas, and the wizard was just an old fake. "Home," she would say.

But when she pictured the sofa—the old green sofa, where her mother and father sat watching TV—who was sitting there? With her feet planted squarely on the floor, with her hands crossed primly in her lap, with her eyeglasses on?

Guida said, "Tara, slow down."

"This car can take it," said Tara. "It's not the piece of junk I had thought."

"Please slow down right now."

"I don't have to. I have extrasensory perception when it comes to police."

"It's getting windy," said Guida.

"That's not the wind," said Tara. "That's me."

Could a Buick do ninety, ninety-five? If a cruiser was hiding on the side in some bushes and came tearing out after her, would she try to outrun it? What would that be like?

"Slow *down*," said Guida.

"I don't want to!" cried Tara, and Guida touched her lightly on the knee, as if she'd lift Tara's leg off the gas pedal.

"It's not my rental I'm worried about," said Guida. "And it's not you, either. It's Mr. Dunfee. He's right behind us in your Mustang, and as soon as you started speeding up, so did he. That sign of yours might not be as tight as you think, or as strong, in spite of being made by Italians, and what if the wind blows it over?"

Tara looked in the rearview mirror. "Guida! That's my car!"

Eighteen

A low-hanging fog had settled over the valley, with a smell of the river and the factories, but the air was as sharp as if it had already turned to winter.

Late autumn on White Cliffs Hill Road used to be so—what was it?

Guida was determined to put her finger on what her life had been like before now, in the saddest time of the year. What exactly had it always been like before?

Disconsolate? As sad as if her heart were made of brick? As alone as if no one else were in the world, and music should be playing in the background, like music for a funeral?

By day it was rich, it was boisterous. The trees blazed with color, and the blue of the sky was as blue as blue could get. The firs of White Cliffs Hill Road stood up against the sky and never looked so green, and the oaks were filled with leaves that looked as if they'd been made, every one, out of bronze, each one in the color of a penny; and in Guida's yard, the sunlight was yellow and lavish and lustrous, all day, and the crows kept squawking and screaming and fighting with the bees for the ripe, ripe pears off Guida's tree.

And just down the road, there had always been White Cliffs. In fall sunlight, it was as white as a wedding cake. The hay fields around it were all blond, like hair. Delivery trucks went by all day:

the Gallaghers had always been lucky in booking the banquet room for the holidays, all through late fall and up to New Year's. It was their busiest time of year and Guida's too, and she knew she had nothing to complain about when it came to being busy.

And then it would be twilight, and then it would be night. And the twilights kept getting shorter and shorter.

She would sit in a chair in her parlor near the heating vent that went down in a chute to her furnace: and it would be silent, silent. Sometimes she did some sewing, and sometimes she turned on the TV, though not that often. Sometimes she'd watch the lights going out at White Cliffs, the way stars go out in the morning.

Sometimes she looked over her bookings to make sure that everyone had paid her. Sometimes she read a book she'd gotten from the library. Sometimes she wrote a letter, in the Italian that was left to her, to the cousin of Coochie Mastromatteo who lived in Naples, and was elderly, and sometimes she wrapped up a package of chocolate to go with it. Sometimes she wrote a letter to a nursing home or one of her customers to say "thank you for the very nice meal." Sometimes she turned on the radio. Sometimes it took a long time for a night to be over.

The leaves would start falling; twilight would last for only half an hour, for twenty minutes, for ten. She'd look forward to the noise of the day.

It was a thing a minute in the daytime and the phone rang often. Late autumn made people feel nervous, with its rushing approach of the holidays, which, for many of Guida's customers, was the same as being outdoors in a field somewhere, quite alone, with a tornado rising up on the horizon.

And nothing could stop it and nothing could be done about it: and then you're standing there with wind in your ears and you're head over heels, as light as a popsicle stick, being blown around in circles, and ending up who knows where. That was Christmas. Thanksgiving was always a little calmer.

It would go on and on, it was like this every year, with days that filled up all around her, filled everything up; she hardly noticed how fast the hours rushed by.

Could the Signora please make an appointment with a new lady at the nursing home, she had a husband who committed suicide a year ago, on Christmas Eve?

Could the Signora come and tell us, please, will the airplane get into a crash, the one we'll be riding, for one thousand dollars on credit, all the way across America to my husband's family in Colorado, for a Thanksgiving dinner that all comes out of cans, even the turkey, and that family hates not only me, but also my husband, and if you come and say the plane will be crashing, we won't go? We tell them, "We're dying to see you, but the fortune-teller told us not to come."

Could the Signora give the county an extra few days this year at the hospital?

Could the Signora come to the jail and sit down with a boy that robbed a convenience store, armed, but he didn't use the gun, and he is nineteen years old, and he just got it into his head that there's no "I'll Be Home for Christmas" in prison?

Could the Signora tell me how to keep my girl off drugs, when it's Christmas that's always the worst, and the rehab places will all be filled? Could the Signora please tell us now, will my father with liver failure stay with us till Christmas Day, or should we put on Christmas early, and take the risk of having it twice?

Could the Signora look into the past—can you tell me, when he told me he loved me, if he lied? Could the Signora look into the future and say if he will love me tomorrow, and what about the day after that?

It had always been at its worst in late fall and she only knew it now—the stillness, the sense in her ears that she could hear falling leaves, even with the windows all shut. She would look at the pear tree in her yard, the crabapple tree, the grass, the leftover bit of a birdbath that everyone always thought was a grave, and the night would come down like a robber—and she would not understand why it happened to her that her heart felt all wrong in her chest.

She would say to herself, "I know too many things about too many people." She would say to herself, "I think I am sick of my job."

She'd pour herself a glass of brandy, maybe two, but never three. She knew from her customers what happened when you started to reach for the bottle as if reaching for a hand, or an arm, or the breasts or the hair of someone who was standing beside you, or the side of their face, or their mouth.

It did not seem right to Guida that she should look back on all those years in her house and think of no better thing to be happy about, beyond, "I lived alone my whole life and I did not become an alcoholic," and, "I always loved the stillness of my house." But that's what she was doing.

What she'd listened to, she now knew, all those years, was the sound of what it's like when something all around you is empty, even though it seems to be full. That sound had always been loudest on nights just like this one, foggy and cold, in late fall, long after twilight was over.

Was that true, all those years? Didn't she love her house, hadn't she fixed it up the way she wanted it? Every penny she'd ever earned went into her house!

All right, she'd admit it, the exterior was in need of repairing: the roof had loose shingles, the gutters were almost falling off their screws, the front porch was getting shaky, and some of the boards contained some rot, but inside, wasn't it good the way it was, with the silence of good wood and beautiful things, and everything in its place, exactly the way she wanted it? It seemed to Guida that her house had never sounded as still or as empty as it did right then, in the moment before Tara walked into it.

Well, not walked in, not exactly. Tara could not have cared less that Guida couldn't remember the last time someone stepped foot in her house who was not a workman or a cleaner or someone making deliveries. Was this the first time Guida had invited someone in? It felt like it.

"Guida!" cried Tara.

She didn't come in lightly, or tentatively, or slowly, or shyly, as anyone else might have done when entering a house they've never been in before, especially when the person who lived there was not in the habit of inviting other people inside.

Tara wasn't pausing in the short front hallway to look around, as Guida would have expected. She had switched on the lights already.

She wasn't looking around in the light at the beautiful wood paneling on all the walls, or the dining room table with its white linen tablecloth that went almost all the way to the floor, or the sideboard full of china and silver, or the shiny oak stairway that might have seemed too wide for a house this small, or the red Persian runner with hardly a spot that was worn, as no one used the stairs except herself, or the armchair in the corner of the parlor, or the French doors at the other end, leading to the dining room, with glass so clean it looked invisible.

Tara came charging in, as if she'd been in Guida's house a thousand times. The screen door rattled behind her. No one had ever let it slam like that before.

Over her head, almost touching it, the ceiling light shook. The fixture was a simple glass dome, and dangling down from it, all around the rim, were smooth shards of crystal in the shape of icicles—like long crystal earrings, or like crystal on a miniature version of an expensive chandelier. Guida had bought the icicles one by one, whenever she had saved enough cash, from a jewelry store at the mall. It had taken about six years to have them all; no more could fit. The icicles had never clattered into each other as they were doing right now, all chimey and tinkling, but Tara didn't notice that, either.

"The inside of your house looks like the inside of White Cliffs," she wasn't saying.

"Guida! You go out there right now and talk to that poor old man! You can't let him just drive off when he came all this way! Go tell him to come in! He hasn't got any money! He did his job! You go out there right now!" Out in the road, with the fog all around, Mr. Dunfee stood by the Mustang as if someone were taking his picture. He had taken off his cap, and he squinted up at the front porch light and waved the cap in the air, like a jockey. Guida waved back.

"He doesn't want to come in," said Guida.

"He has to eat!" cried Tara. "He can't be driving all the way back in one night, and it's foggy!"

"I don't think he'll drive back tonight," said Guida, "now that we've brought him back to town. He'll want to go visit his old friends."

"Then you have to pay him! He did his job! You hired him!"

"But Tara, I gave him my car."

"That wasn't pay! He has to have something to drive! He's doing you a favor!"

The keys to the old Toyota were in Mr. Dunfee's hand. Five minutes ago, out at the end of the driveway, it had occurred to Guida to sign over the title to him. She'd written up a bill of sale for him, too, for one dollar, which she refused to accept, when he took out his wallet to give her one.

The pen he'd given her to use was the one he'd used before, back at the cottage. She had not invited Harold in. The bill of sale was on the back of the envelope from the rental car company. Nothing involving Mr. Dunfee needed to transpire inside her house.

"Signora," Mr. Dunfee had said, "and Signorina, you also. I will never forget this day."

Tara had been a model of restraint and self-control for about five minutes. She'd been standing beside Guida, a little more closely than she had to. She was not looking down the road to the hazy fog that had covered White Cliffs Hill. It was the same as if White Cliffs Hill weren't there. Tara had been looking out the sides of her eyes at that poor little Celica—a little bit rusty, and a little worn and creaky—sitting in Guida's driveway as if abandoned forever, and not only abandoned, but *lied* about. She didn't look at Guida's car like something she felt sorry for. She looked at it as if Guida's offer to give it away was the best idea Guida had ever had. She looked at it as if she wanted Mr. Dunfee to drive it to a wrecking yard, as if Mr. Dunfee should have been paid to remove it.

She'd said, politely, "I just have one small comment, Guida."

She was not implying that Guida's old car was so old and so square and so rusty that, once he drove it away, Mr. Dunfee might get only get a couple of miles before the floor caved in and fell away, and he'd find himself with his feet coming out of the bottom, running along the middle of a road, just like Fred Flintstone, except the tires of the Celica weren't stone.

"I cannot believe I just came all the way home with you, Guida, never mind just spent a whole day with you, and never mind everything else, and I'm standing here, and the thing you have in your driveway looks like Fred Flintstone's car."

"I'm sorry," Guida had answered. That was when she went into the house.

ELLEN COONEY   215 ⏤

She had turned on all the lights. Tara was shouting at Mr. Dunfee from the doorway, telling him to wait, she had something to give him, and Guida went over to her armchair, and nearly fell into it backward.

It had been a long, long, long day. Her stockings were all baggy; her skirt had never dried all the way from being sogged through with wet flowers in sodden, tissue-paper wrappers; it seemed that flinty little bits of pebbles from the rock she'd sat on had in fact embedded the wool of her skirt, and might never come out. Her blouse felt as limp as if it had just come out of a washing machine, on the spin cycle, even though it was silk.

All the same, she was wondering, "What's going to happen next?" It was late. There was only one bed in the house. Her legs felt like legs made of jelly.

"Guida! What are you sitting down for! You give Mr. Dunfee some money right now before he's gone! You give him money for gas, and money for doing his job! I happen to have an interest in jobs! You don't hire someone for a job and not pay them!"

"All right, all right." It wasn't that Guida begrudged Harold Dunfee; she wasn't miserly. She'd really felt that the Celica was payment enough. Her purse was on the little table in the hall. "Hand me my purse, please," said Guida.

Tara grabbed it and threw it at her, just hauled back her arm and threw it—Guida's good brown leather purse with its handsome gold clasp, thrown through the air like a football—and it landed with a plop at Guida's feet.

Tara came into the parlor just behind it, almost on tiptoes, but not quite: her head would have bumped the ceiling. "Sorry, I thought you would catch it," she said.

Guida bent to pick up her purse. Her hands on the clasp were shaky. Nothing was broken; her glasses were in a metal case with

THE WHITE PALAZZO

heavy lining, intact. She opened the case and took out the glasses to check them before she handed Tara her wallet.

Why wasn't she noticing the way Guida had fixed up her house? The wood in her parlor was as brown as cooked chestnuts, and as smooth to the touch as marble. The lamplight was like candlelight; there was not one speck of dust. But Tara noticed nothing, as if she'd been looking at these things all her life.

"You only have eleven dollars, Guida."

"Tell him we'll owe him more."

"I'll be right back." Again the front door shook as she slammed it, and the light in the hallway clinked madly, as if it never would stop.

One day, out on White Cliffs Hill Road, just a few hundred feet from Guida's house, a repair truck showed up from the electric company, and a man in a bucket at the end of the crane worked all day on the wires.

It had been autumn then, too, but earlier; the trees the crane poked up through had barely started changing. Guida went out there because she knew the man in the bucket, although his face was partly obscured by his hardhat. His name was Junior Schell. She did seeings for his mother all the time.

The hardhat was bright yellow, the sky was blue. Junior was handsome and tan. He made it seem as if standing high up in the air at the end of a crane was something he'd been born to do, and it crossed her mind that she'd like to find out what that was like, but she never got into the bucket. She never even asked.

A change came into the air—into her ears—and it stunned her so much, all she could do was shake her head and call up to Junior, "What just happened?" She knew that the sound she was hearing was from the wires, but she couldn't make out what it was.

"Buzz just went dead," was Junior's answer. "That's what I was out here to do. Damn near drove everyone crazy in your neighborhood, considering the complaints."

And sure enough, as soon as it was gone, Guida realized that for days, perhaps weeks, there'd been a strange, high-tension electrical buzzing in the air all the time, like a steady background humming of insects. Something had been wrong with the wires. She knew exactly what it was, when it stopped.

That was what happened to her house when Tara came into it, and it wasn't just because Tara was screaming at her and shaking everything up. Guida heard the sound of what she had been listening to, all those years, when it stopped.

"Mr. Dunfee! We owe you, big time!" cried Tara in the driveway.

"The crows are going to love her," thought Guida. "They'll learn from her to be a hundred times worse than they are. I will never have a minute of peace. They'll learn from her they'll never have to be quiet again in the nighttime, just because it's night."

She wondered what her neighbors would think of Tara's sign. There must have been a switch for the electronics inside the Mustang; it wasn't lit up. Still, it wasn't something anyone wouldn't notice.

"Guida!" cried Tara. She didn't come up to the porch. She yelled from where she was. The walls could have been wide open. They could have been made of cardboard.

Guida reached over to the window that looked out on the driveway. She could reach it just fine from her chair. She pulled back the curtain—it was her best silk drape, as white as when your breath shows in winter. She handled it carefully because her hands felt so raw and so rough, and why wouldn't they?

"Guida! Can you cook?" cried Tara.

Guida shook her head in the window, and Tara cried out to Mr.

Dunfee, "OK! Come back tomorrow! Seven o'clock! Come for dinner! We'll get takeout!"

Guida sighed and said to herself, "She is going to fill my kitchen with things no one would eat unless they were twenty-four years old." She leaned back in her chair. She wondered if she had food in her kitchen right now. She didn't know; she couldn't remember.

Her feet were planted squarely on the floor. Her arms were on the arms of the chair. Her glasses were in her hand as if she'd been wearing them, as if she had just taken them off, the way she always did when she'd finished a seeing.

"Bye Mr. Dunfee! See you tomorrow night!" cried Tara.

The engine of the old Toyota sputtered. It was working. Guida didn't have to go out there and give Mr. Dunfee the rental. She listened. In five seconds, Tara would come charging back inside, and already, the front door was trembling in its frame, as if gearing itself up to be flung back and rattled, as if it were something alive. Maybe it was. Maybe everything in the house was alive now, with ears and eyes and a memory, or maybe it had all been sleeping, and was just now waking up. That was what it felt like—the walls, the wood, the carpets, the lights, the tables, the chairs, everything. Everything was just now waking up.

"I'm back," said Tara. She stood above Guida like a tower. She stretched out her back, as a cat does, and then her arms, as if she'd just awakened, too. "Guida, I'm back," she said. "And I'm *starving*."

COLOPHON

The White Palazzo was designed at Coffee House Press
in the Warehouse District of downtown Minneapolis.
The text is set in Caslon.